NO VACANCY

NO VACANCY

Tziporah Cohen

Groundwood Books
House of Anansi Press
Toronto / Berkeley

Groundwood Books / House of Anansi Press
groundwoodbooks.com

Groundwood Books respectfully acknowledges that the land on which we operate is
the Traditional Territory of many Nations, including the Anishinabeg, the Wendat
and the Haudenosaunee. It is also the Treaty Lands of the Mississaugas of the Credit.

We gratefully acknowledge for their financial support of our publishing
program the Canada Council for the Arts, the Ontario Arts Council and
the Government of Canada.

 Canada Council **Conseil des Arts**
for the Arts **du Canada**

 ONTARIO ARTS COUNCIL
CONSEIL DES ARTS DE L'ONTARIO
an Ontario government agency
un organisme du gouvernement de l'Ontario

With the participation of the Government of Canada
Avec la participation du gouvernement du Canada | Canadä

Library and Archives Canada Cataloguing in Publication
Title: No vacancy / Tziporah Cohen.
Names: Cohen, Tziporah, author.
Identifiers: Canadiana (print) 20190229950 | Canadiana (ebook) 20190229969
| ISBN 9781773064109 (hardcover) | ISBN 9781773064116 (EPUB) | ISBN
9781773064123 (Kindle)
Classification: LCC PS8605.O3788 N62 2020 | DDC jC813/.6—dc23

Jacket design by Michael Solomon
Jacket illustration by Sam Kalda

Groundwood Books is a Global Certified Accessible™ (GCA by Benetech) publisher.
An ebook version of this book that meets stringent accessibility standards is available
to students and readers with print disabilities.

Groundwood Books is committed to protecting our natural environment. This book
is made of material from well-managed FSC®-certified forests, recycled materials,
and other controlled sources.

Printed and bound in Canada

MIX
Paper from
responsible sources
FSC® C016245

For Max, Dalit and Adina

1

Town of Greenvale
Population 510

The green road sign goes by so fast I'm not even sure I read it right.

"Seriously?" I say. "Did that sign say Population 510?" There are practically more people than that on the block where we live.

Where we used to live.

"What sign?" says Dad.

"I need to pee again," I say. I weaseled a Coke out of Dad at the last rest stop and now I'm paying the price.

"We'll be there in two minutes," Mom says as Dad turns off the highway onto a service road. It's the first thing she's said in about a hundred miles.

Dad turns down a tree-lined street and then another and stops suddenly in front of another sign. Sammy is asleep in his car seat. I tickle his feet through his socks, and his eyelids flutter but he doesn't wake up.

This sign is a faded yellow with The Jewel Motor Inn painted in red letters with a black outline. Some of the paint has worn off and the wood underneath shows through. The weeds under the sign are tall enough to tickle the bottom of the *J*.

On the top someone has taped a smaller sign made of cardboard: Closed. Reopening Monday, July 6.

Today is Monday, June 29.

Dad turns into the entrance and stops halfway into the parking lot next to a little playground that's really just two busted swings and one of those painted metal horses on a giant spring from the olden days. There's a sandbox, though even from the car I can see it's full of weeds and garbage.

The playground around the corner from our old apartment in the middle of the city is bigger than this one. A lot bigger.

Dad parks in front of a two-story building the color of dried mustard. Mom sighs and he leans over to give her a kiss.

"Here's to new beginnings," he says. Mom sighs again. I don't think she likes new beginnings.

Seeing the Jewel Motor Inn up close, I'm not sure I do either. Though it's not like I have a choice. After Dad lost his job, we had to give up our apartment and now my two best friends will be five hours away and having a new beginning without me.

Dad gives me a big smile — the kind adults give you when they're trying to make you feel something they don't.

"Welcome home," he says.

Mom and Dad get out of the car and tell me to stay with Sammy, who is still sound asleep, his head tilted to one side and his lips pursed like he's dreaming about kissing, even though he's only two and a half years old.

I open my door and stand next to the car so I can get a better look at my new home. The hot, muggy air outside feels like the air in the city but smells different. Greener, I guess.

On the first floor, right in front of our parking spot, is a glass door with Reception painted on it in faded letters. There are two big planters on either side of the door filled with dried-out brown plants.

Mom comes out the door. A bell jingles when it opens. She reaches into the car and grabs her phone.

"I have to pee," I tell her.

"Stay with Sammy, please, Miriam," Mom says. She shuts the car door too hard and Sammy wakes up.

"Out," he says, rubbing his eyes and looking at me. "Out."

I reach over and squeeze his chubby little hand three times for "I love you," like Grandma taught me when I was little. When I unbuckle him he climbs into the front seat and pretends to drive. I scramble into the passenger seat to make sure he doesn't honk the horn.

He's lucky. He's too young to have real friends to leave behind. He didn't care about leaving his room or his school or his favorite teacher. His whole world is still with him.

"Come, Sammy." He grabs my hand and we head into Reception just as Mom and Dad come out. I peek behind them. The room is empty.

"Where are the people who are supposed to show us everything?" I ask.

"No one's here," Dad says, frowning. "They left."

Mom starts taking things out of the trunk: Sammy's stroller, a cooler of sandwiches and snacks, two small suitcases for me and Sammy and a big one for her and Dad. The rest of our stuff is coming later in a truck.

"They left?" I'm confused. The previous owners were supposed to stay here with us for a week and teach us everything about running a motel.

Mom slams the trunk hard. Sammy lets go of my hand and starts to run out into the parking lot. Dad grabs him and holds him upside down and tickles the part of his belly sticking out over his diaper.

His giggle is the only sound for what seems like a million years.

Dad stays in the parking lot, yelling at someone on his cell phone, while Sammy and I follow Mom back into Reception. I can smell chlorine, and it reminds me of the Y back home where Lekha had her birthday party last month. I still haven't totally forgiven her for having a pool party when she knew how I felt about water. I ended up helping her mom set up for the cake while everyone was splashing around and having fun.

13

I follow Mom around the high counter, taking in the computer behind it. There's a desk against the back wall and next to it a closed door with a sign that says Office. And next to that there's a bathroom, thank God.

Back home, my best friends, Dahlia and Lekha, and I have a public bathroom rating system. Most of the bathrooms in the city are a one or two out of ten, usually tiny and dirty and smelly, with toilet paper on the floor and paper towel dispensers that are empty or jammed. Then there are the ones in fancy restaurants, the ones we go to for special occasions, which get an eight or a nine because they're big, with art on the walls and automatic faucets and blasting hand dryers that actually dry your hands instead of just moving the water around.

This bathroom? I give it a four because it's clean, but it's still tiny, and the toilet seat is chipped. And the soap dispenser is filled with bright pink liquid that looks like diarrhea medicine.

When I come out, Sammy's climbing onto one of the two old couches that face each other in the middle of the room, a scratched-up coffee table between them.

"Mi-wam," he calls to me.

The couches are greenish brown with frayed edges and there's a rip down the back of one of them. I try not to think about the dirt and sit down, and Sammy snuggles against me until he spies the display stand near the front door. It's filled with colorful pamphlets, the only thing in the room that's not dull and dreary.

Sammy toddles right over and starts pulling them out one by one and dropping them on the floor. I pick them up and try to put them back into their slots but he is way faster than I am so I give up and look at them instead. *Crystal Caverns*, says one, with photos of a huge cave filled with shiny rock icicles that hang from the ceiling. It's magical.

I find a booklet called *Places to Stay in the Finger Lakes Region*. I look inside but the Jewel Motor Inn isn't listed.

At the very top of the display, too high for Sammy to reach, there's an ad for Mabel's Diner, which is right next door to the Jewel. The ad says that kids ten and under eat breakfast free and that there are unlimited coffee refills.

Since I just turned eleven and hate even the smell of coffee, I'm not impressed.

Sammy grabs another pamphlet and hands it to me. There's a map of upstate New York on one side and a map of Greenvale on the other. He heads for a door on the far side of the room across from the desk, which says Pool. That explains the chlorine smell. I can see the water through the grimy glass. Just the sight of it makes my heart beat faster.

I scoop Sammy up. He squirms and says, "Dow, dow," but I hold onto him tight.

"How are we going to know what to do if the last owners aren't here to show us?" I ask.

"Not a good time for questions, Miriam," says Mom, rubbing the scar on her palm — something she does when she's stressed. She searches for something behind the counter as the bell jingles and Dad comes in.

Before they decided to move here, my parents had a big fight right in front of me. Mom said that a week wasn't nearly enough, that running a motel wasn't something you picked up overnight. She said it was a whole new *skill set*, and that some people went to college for four years to learn how to do it.

"It's not the Ritz-Carlton," Dad said to her then. "It's just answering the phone and cleaning up after people. How hard could that be?"

That made Mom stomp off talking to herself about marketing and supply inventory and cash flow and about how no one could even clean up after themselves in our apartment in New York City. She didn't talk to Dad the whole rest of that day.

But then he did his magic with her, and they made up, and here we are.

Mom gives Dad the eyes of death. The magic has clearly worn off. She comes out from behind the counter holding up a small plastic card.

"Let's get your suitcase and go see your room," she says to me. "Room 109."

Room 109. The room I'll share with Sammy.

Because as of today, I — Miriam Brockman, formerly of New York City — live in a motel in Greenvale, New York.

Population 514.

2

We have to go outside to get to Room 109, which is kind of weird. Apparently that's what makes this a motel and not a hotel, where you get to the rooms from the inside. Here you can just drive your car right up to the door of your room, like you're in a rush to get in.

Which seems unlikely, given what I've seen so far.

Room 109 is almost at the end of the strip. Room 110, which Mom says will be for her and Dad, is at the end.

Mom shows me how to stick the key card into the slot on the door. When the red light above the slot turns green, she pushes and the door opens with a click.

"Surprisingly modern," she says, chuckling. It's good to hear her laugh.

The smell hits me before anything else: a mix of wet dog, old sneakers and the stuff Dad uses to get stains out of the rug at home. The room is so dark I can't see a thing.

I flip the light switch and the ceiling light goes on, but that hardly makes a difference.

Mom pulls aside the thick brown curtains. Light pours in.

"That's better," she says. "What do you think?"

I stayed in a hotel once when I was eight and Grandma took me to Disney World. The room we stayed in was huge, with big tall beds that I practically needed a ladder to climb into. Those beds were clouds, with piles of marshmallow pillows. That room had thick, squishy carpet that made my feet feel like king and queen of the floor. The bathroom was practically as big as my bedroom back home, and next to the sink were little lavender soaps that looked and smelled like flowers.

And the towels? They were the biggest, softest towels you can imagine.

That bathroom was a definite ten. Maybe even an eleven.

In Room 109, the only thing that squishes under my feet is a wadded-up tissue that someone left on the floor. The carpet feels hard and thin under my sandals and there are only two pillows — one on each bed — and they're as flat as peppermint patties. There are soaps in the bathroom but they're just boring rectangles covered in white paper and don't have any smell at all.

I put a towel to my face. Scratchy.

I give the bathroom a five since there's a bathtub, at least.

"Look," says Mom, showing me the door that connects this room to theirs. Their room has one big bed in it instead of two. Mom says I can leave the door open, to make it feel like one apartment, or close it when I want some privacy.

"Privacy," I say, and close it, even though Mom is in the room with us.

Sammy wants it open.

"No pi-cy," he shouts, running back and forth between the two rooms, crashing from one bed to the other.

"Ice bucket!" Mom says, holding up an orange

plastic container. "There's an ice machine at the end of the strip."

As if that's supposed to make everything better.

I sit on the end of the bed by the window — which I've already decided will be my bed — and stare at the dust in the sunbeams. The dust doesn't dance around like normal dust. This dust just hangs there, like it's stuck.

The window won't open for me no matter how hard I try. Mom fights with it until she gets it unstuck.

I stare through the grimy screen at the parking lot, empty except for our car. It's not the New York skyline, that's for sure.

"I'll take Sammy for a bit," says Mom. "You can unpack your things and when you find your mezuzah we'll put it on the door. Make it feel a little more like home."

Like home? Yeah, right.

Mom takes Sammy through the connecting door into Room 110. The door to the outside is still open, hopefully letting in more fresh air.

I throw myself down on the bed, which squeaks like some kind of giant mouse, and stare at the walls, which are painted a color that is sort of halfway between macaroni and cheese and rotting bananas.

There are darker rectangles on the wall above each bed, where some art must have hung once.

Then I notice the TV on the dresser. A TV in my room!

Back in our apartment, we had one TV, in the living room where Mom and Dad could see what I was watching. TVs were one hundred percent not allowed in the bedroom.

I grab the remote from the bedside table. I flip through what turns out to be three channels: news, a soap opera and baby cartoons. No cable or Netflix.

I sigh. At least Sammy will have something to watch.

I pull out the photos that I stuck in the outside pocket of my suitcase. There's one of me and Dahlia and Lekha at the skating rink at Rockefeller Center, wearing pom-pom hats, our arms around each other's shoulders. The three of us are making faces at the camera. I push it into the corner of the frame of the cracked mirror that sits on the dresser at the front of the room. I want to call them and tell them what a dump the Jewel Motor Inn is, but Lekha's at sleepaway camp with no phone and Dahlia's staying with her grandparents in Israel for most of the summer and I don't know their number.

Dahlia and I are practically the only kids in all of Manhattan that don't have their own cell phones.

Were. I keep forgetting I don't live there anymore.

I rummage through my suitcase looking for the piece of paper where I wrote Lekha's camp address and find my mezuzah tucked next to it. I turn the pretty metal case over in my hand and lift the flap to see the piece of parchment inside, where there are words written from the Torah that Jews are supposed to put on the doorposts in their homes. I stick it back in the suitcase and take out Lekha's address.

When I leave the room to go see if Dad has any paper I can use for a letter, the door closes behind me with a loud click and the red light turns back on. I try the handle but the door is locked shut and the key card is inside.

A mezuzah won't be nearly enough to make this place feel like home.

Dad gives me a pad of paper that says The Jewel Motor Inn at the top, then hands me my own key card for Room 109. He punches a hole in the corner and loops a rubber band into it so I can wear it around my wrist.

Instead of unpacking or writing to Lekha, I lie down on the hard bed and study the stains and cracks on the ceiling, hoping to find one that's in the shape of a rabbit, like in *Madeline*, my favorite book when I was little.

There isn't.

I give up and get up to inspect the dresser. It has six drawers. I'm supposed to save two for Sammy's stuff. That leaves four for me, which isn't nearly enough. To make things worse, the top drawer on the left is stuck closed.

I'm pulling on it when there's a knock on the open door.

"Hola!"

The woman in the doorway is wearing jeans and a T-shirt. A ring of keys and a couple of key cards dangle from one hand. There's a cross on a chain around her neck, made of a white stone that sparkles when the sun hits it from the window. It's beautiful, like her.

"Sorry," I say, giving the drawer one last yank and turning toward her. "The motel doesn't open until next week. We just got here."

"Then you must be the family who bought the

Jewel! *Bienvenida*." The words roll one after the other off her tongue. "I'm Maria."

"I'm Miriam."

"Miriam," she says. *"Que lindo."*

I know she's speaking Spanish because I heard it a lot back in the city, but aside from recognizing a couple of words on signs, I don't understand it.

"What a beautiful name," she says when I just look at her.

She explains to me that she works at the motel, cleaning rooms and doing whatever else needs to be done. Dad paid her to stay on while the motel was closed and to keep working here when we took over.

Mom walks in through the connecting door and I introduce them.

"Bienvenida," says Maria as she steps forward to shake Mom's hand.

Mom takes a good look at Maria's necklace and rubs her palm.

"Maria used to work for the old owners and Dad asked her to stay," I tell her.

"We appreciate that," Mom says. "Do you have the key to the storage room?" She's speaking a bit more slowly than usual.

"Which key?" asks Maria.

"The key," Mom repeats, saying the words louder and even slower, like she thinks Maria is deaf or stupid. "To … the … storage … room."

Maria inspects her big ring of keys. She takes one off and hands it to my mother.

"This one's a master. It opens the storage room, the laundry room, the office — just about everything except the guest rooms. I can get a copy made for you later if you want."

Mom's face turns pink. She nods, takes the key and heads back into her room.

"Las llaves," Maria says to me, holding up the rest of the ring. "Keys. In Spanish."

"Las llaves," I repeat.

She steps over to my dresser, grasps the handle of the stuck drawer and yanks downward on it. It slides open.

"Bienvenida," Maria says again. "Welcome." She winks at me as she turns to leave.

I can't help but wink back. Her smile is about the only thing really welcoming about this place.

—

After I unpack my clothes into all four drawers, I go exploring. Sammy trails along until I get frustrated with how slow he is and pick him up.

Rooms 101 through 110 are on the first floor. Some of the numbers on the doors have come loose and are upside down, so that Room 109 looks like Room 106, with the six hanging down like it's going to jump off and run away. There's a vending machine between Rooms 102 and 103, partly filled with bags of chips and candy bars.

I take an outdoor staircase to the right of Room 110, my parents' room, up to the second floor, where Rooms 111 to 119 open onto a kind of outdoor hallway-balcony. Sammy's getting heavy so I put him down and he walk-runs down the strip of carpet between the doors and the cement balcony wall.

"Me, me," he says, pounding his little fists on another vending machine, this one filled just with sodas.

I lean over the balcony. I can see the diner next door, the one from the ad. Down below is the empty parking lot, the dinky playground, and the trees lining the side of the road that I saw on the drive in. I hear the swish of trucks as they fly by on the highway behind the motel, even though I can't see them.

What happened to all the green fields and forests and farms that we drove by on the way here?
I thought Greenvale would look more like Central
Park. This looks more like my old Playmobil playground set, with half the pieces missing.

I take Sammy down the stairs at the other end,
him babbling at me the whole way about something
even I can't understand, and come out right in front
of Reception.

Dad's at the computer and barely looks up when
the bell jingles. I ignore the gross couches and the
door to the pool. At the back of the room, a flight of
stairs — this one indoors — goes up to the dining
room, which is where guests get free breakfast. Next
to the stairs is a small elevator. Sammy gets excited
when he sees it but there are no buttons, just a place
for a key. Service Elevator, the sign on it says.

The dining room is pretty cool. Lots of small
tables and chairs in the middle, with ice and juice
machines against one wall, labeled Ice and Orange
and Apple. Everything is labeled here. There are two
giant thermoses, Coffee and Hot Water, a big toaster
that can fit six pieces of bread at once and, best of
all, a waffle maker labeled Waffles. In case it wasn't
obvious.

I try to imagine how the room will look next week, filled with people talking and forks clinking and the smell of waffles and syrup.

"Dwink," says Sammy.

I take a paper cup from the stack next to the juice machine and press the button for Apple. Nothing but rusty-looking water comes out, which I won't give him, which makes him cry. I'm saved by a packet of crackers I find on the counter.

So, nineteen rooms minus one for my parents and one for me and Sammy means seventeen rooms for customers — guests, I'm supposed to call them. The idea, apparently, is that Mom and Dad will run this place for a couple of years, and since we don't have to pay rent, they'll be able to save enough to sell the motel and buy a house. A house with real bedrooms and a backyard, close enough to Manhattan that Mom and Dad can work there and I can still see my friends.

The Jewel's old owners, the ones who left, had to move across the country when the man's mom got sick, so Dad said they sold him the motel at a good price. He told Mom it needed some minor sprucing up, but he didn't think it was anything we couldn't handle.

"Mi-wam?" Sammy pulls at my leg. I pretend-chase him and he toddles away from me as fast as his little legs can go, giggling and leaving a trail of crumbs across the scratched-up floor. He heads right toward a broken chair in the corner with sharp screws sticking out the sides, so I scoop him up again.

This place needs some *major* sprucing up.

Dad said there weren't a lot of options after he lost his job, and he always wanted to live in a small town anyway. Somehow he got Mom to agree to try this for two years.

Two *years*.

I don't think we're going to last two weeks.

3

"Anyone home?"

There's a girl standing in the doorway to reception. She's holding a pie. My stomach rumbles. It's our first morning here and no one's gone to the grocery store yet. Dinner last night was soggy leftover tuna sandwiches, and breakfast this morning was cereal we brought from home, without even milk.

"Are you a guest?" I ask, even though I know she's not because we're not open yet and what kid would come to a motel without parents and holding a pie? I can't get up because my lap is full of invoices that I'm supposed to be putting in order. Someone needs to tell my parents that it's summer vacation.

The girl laughs. "I'm Kate. My grandma runs the diner next door."

"Oh," I say. "I'm Miriam. This is Sammy." I point to my brother who is covering the other couch with blocks. "Your grandma runs Mabel's?"

"Yeah, except her name is Myrna. She sent me over with a welcome pie."

She puts it on the counter. A yummy smell fills the room, covering up the chlorine for once.

"What kind is it?" I ask. It doesn't smell like apple, my favorite.

"Guess," Kate says.

"Blueberry," I guess, looking at the purple stain on her T-shirt.

"Nope."

"Plum?"

"Nope," says Kate again. "Grape! Grandma's specialty."

"You can make pies from grapes?"

"You'll love it. Grandma makes the best grape pies in the county. She won first prize in the county fair three years in a row. They even wrote about it in the paper."

I try to imagine someone's grandmother's pie making it into the newspaper back home. I can't.

Kate plops down next to me on the couch, sending a pile of sorted invoices to the floor.

"Shoot," she says, as Mom comes out of the office.

"Finally got that miserable printer to work," Mom says, actually smiling. She sees the pie on the counter. "This smells heavenly."

"It's a grape pie," I tell her, gathering the invoices off the floor. "Kate's grandmother, whose name is Myrna but owns Mabel's Diner, makes them."

Mom turns to Kate. "Please tell her thank you, Kate. And sorry we haven't gone over yet to meet her."

"Are you going to church on Sunday? We always eat lunch at the diner after. Mom said to ask you to come. Maria always comes too, and Father Donovan."

There's an awkward silence and then Mom says, "I don't think so. We don't go to church."

Kate looks surprised. "Really?"

"We're Jewish," I say.

"Seriously?" says Kate, looking me up and down. "I've never had a Jewish friend before."

My face gets hot.

Mom clears her throat. "It's good to meet you, Kate, and please thank your grandmother for the pie, but we've got a ton of work to do if we're going to open in less than a week."

"No problem," says Kate, hopping up. "See you later!" The bell jingles and she's gone.

Mom exhales slowly.

"When you're done with the invoices, Miriam, your dad could use some help with inventory in the dining room."

"Honestly, Mom," I say. I could hardly sleep last night and I need a nap. It's way too quiet here, even with the window open. No honking horns or police sirens. Just the sound of crickets and cars on the highway and Sammy tossing in the other bed, behind the bed rail Dad put up so he doesn't fall out.

"Teamwork," Mom says, tossing me a box of paper clips.

I open my mouth to tell her that my two best friends are having fun this summer while I'm sorting invoices, but she shoots me an End-of-Discussion look and goes back into the office.

This team member just wants to go home.

After two hours of counting, I'm still tired but now I'm starving too. Mom gives me a ten-dollar bill and sends me over to the diner.

Signs in the window advertise Breakfast All Day! and Homemade Concord Grape Pies!

34

A bell rings when I open the door, just like at Reception.

"Yoo-hoo! In the kitchen," a voice calls.

"Hello?" I say.

A woman wearing a blue-stained apron comes out of the back.

"Oh, I thought you were Kate," she says. "You must be Miriam. Kate told me about you. Welcome! I'm Myrna Whitley." She sticks out her hand.

"Hi," I say, shaking it. "Why is the diner called Mabel's if your name is Myrna?"

She has a low, rumbly laugh. "Sign company confused two jobs. There's a woman in Spartanburg named Mabel who goes to work every day at Myrna's Hair Salon. They said they could fix it or I could keep the mistake for free. Everyone around here knows my name anyway."

She waves me into a booth.

"You guys must be busy next door. With the motel being closed for the past month, there must be a lot to get ready. Can I make you some lunch?"

"That's what Mom sent me here for." I show her the ten-dollar bill. "Oh, and she says thanks for the pie. She's saving it for dinner."

"You can put your money away. Today's lunch is on me. Grilled cheese is Mr. Whitley's specialty, if you like that."

Sounds good to me. "With tomato?"

"One grilled cheese with tomato coming up," says a man's voice, his head peeking from the window into the kitchen.

"Mr. Whitley does the cooking," Mrs. Whitley says. "Except for the pies. That's my job."

She tilts her head at me. "You know, it's tourist season now and with you guys getting the motel up and running again, I'll need someone to help peel grapes. The local Concord grapes aren't ripe yet, so a truck delivers grapes from California once a week. Kate's at camp during the day so she can't help. You'd be the perfect person, if you want to. We'll have to ask your parents, of course."

"Sure," I say. It sounds like fun, and I'd rather work in a diner than sweep the parking lot or whatever job I'm going to get stuck with next. And I didn't even know you could peel grapes.

Looks like I'm going to learn a new *skill set* too.

4

As it turns out, I don't get back to the diner for the next two days. I spend all my time scrubbing the juice machine and sorting key cards and counting soaps.

My parents start every sentence with, "Miriam, could you ..." or "Miriam, please go get ..." or "Miriam, have you seen ..." Even Sammy's in on it, saying, "Mi-wam" over and over until I pick him up or hand him a toy or tickle him. Maria's the only one who takes the time to answer my questions, and even she doesn't stop moving when she talks.

Mom was right. Running a motel is a ton of work and we don't even have people staying here yet. Every time I try to ask her about working in the diner, I get the eyes of death and chicken out.

Today my job is keeping Sammy out of the way. We did finger paints this morning and I sang him ten rounds of "The Itsy Bitsy Spider," which for some reason cracks him up, and then pushed him on the swing.

Now he's napping so I finally get a break. I'm standing outside in front of the first-floor vending machine, trying to figure out how many people will have to buy Ring Pops before the watermelon one gets to the front. Of course, I could just ask Mom for the key and open the machine and take the one I want, but that would be cheating.

"Hey, squirt!"

I whirl around at the voice. "Uncle Mordy!"

Uncle Mordy drops his giant duffel bag and wraps me in a huge hug.

"I didn't know you were coming," I say when I can breathe again.

"Came to help out. Heard the old owners took off."

He takes his bag and I follow him into Reception.

"How long will you be here? Are you staying in one of the rooms?"

"I'll be here as long as your parents need me, or at least until I have to go back and set up my classroom for the new year. And I didn't bring a tent, so I hope there's a deluxe suite ready for me."

He obviously hasn't had a tour yet.

He drops down onto one of the couches. A small cloud of dust rises around him.

"I'm starving. Anything to eat around here?"

"There's some breakfast stuff upstairs in the little kitchen in the back of the dining room. We can cook there but we don't have our own dining room. We just use the motel one. And Mabel's Diner is next door. Mr. Whitley makes awesome grilled cheese, but he's never heard of challah and makes it from regular bread." I stop, remembering that Uncle Mordy won't eat in a restaurant that isn't kosher.

He reaches into his bag and pulls out two big challahs. No poppy or sesame seeds. Just plain on top, the way I like them.

"Good thing it's Friday," he says. "We'll take the leftovers to him on Sunday and you can show him how to make the real thing."

I tell Uncle Mordy about the grape pies and about my job peeling grapes, which I haven't started yet because Mom says family comes first and they still need my help.

"Grape pie?"

"I know, right? It's even better than apple. And it turns your tongue totally purple. What room are you staying in?"

"No idea. Let's go find your mom and dad and ask."

"And you have to meet Maria."

I'm just about to tell him more about learning Spanish when Mom walks in holding Sammy, who is rubbing his eyes, still half asleep.

"Mordechai! You made good time." She gives him a kiss on the cheek. "You have no idea how glad I am to see —"

Sammy wakes up enough to recognize Uncle Mordy and shrieks, practically leaping out of Mom's arms.

"Mo-dee take poo! Take Sammy poo!"

Uncle Mordy looks horrified.

"He wants you to take him to the pool," I say, being the family expert in Sammy-speak.

"Oh," Uncle Mordy says. "Whew. There's a pool?"

I motion toward the pool door, which I still

haven't been through. "The pool cleaner guy came yesterday so now we can use it but Mom hasn't had time to take him."

Uncle Mordy holds Sammy above his head and Sammy stretches his legs out straight to be an airplane and giggles.

"So, Deborah, should I take my nephew swimming or is there something else you want me to do first? Other than find some lunch."

Mom sinks into the sagging couch. "Oh, Mordy, the pool would be great. Then Miriam can help pick up the trash that's blown all over the parking lot while I make some phone calls. She's been a great help." She pats my knee.

Pick up trash? If I'm forced to work away my summer vacation, why can't I do something that's fun, at least, like take reservations or fill the soda machine?

Mom puts her head back and closes her eyes. "What a mess."

"Have no fear," says Uncle Mordy. "Mordy is here." He turns Sammy upside down over his shoulder and another squeal fills the room.

He grabs his duffel with his free hand and turns to me. "How about you show me the way to that

41

kitchen, Miriam? I need a snack and to get tonight's dinner into the fridge."

I really hope there's some of Uncle Mordy's barbecued chicken in that duffel. When it comes to Shabbat dinner, even grilled cheese won't cut it.

"Hey, squirt, you coming in?"

I finally finished picking up all the disgusting cigarette butts and sticky popsicle sticks and dirty napkins from the parking lot and slipped into the pool room, figuring it's the last place Mom will look to find me and put me to work doing something else.

Sammy is squealing and splashing and trying to grab Uncle Mordy's glasses off his face. I hate that my baby brother is so happy in the water without even trying, when I can't even put my big toe in without freaking out.

"No, thanks," I say from the doorway. "Too cold."

"You can tell from all the way over there?"

"Uh-huh."

"I see," he says, dodging Sammy's hands. He stands him on the side and catches him when he jumps in. I jump back so I won't get splashed, even though there's no way the water can reach me.

I like that Uncle Mordy doesn't pretend the water's really warm or try to splash me or pull me in. I want to tell him so much. How every night since we got here I hear Mom and Dad argue through the wall between our rooms. How I miss my friends. How much I want this motel thing to be a dream that I wake up from and find myself back in our apartment in Manhattan.

"You'll go in when you're ready," he says.

Which will be never. Or maybe longer.

Shabbat starts at sundown, so around six o'clock we all take a break from the cleaning and phone calling and organizing and take showers and put on clean clothes. Uncle Mordy and I put a couple of the little tables together in the middle of the dining room. Our special Shabbat tablecloths are in storage, so Mom covers the tables with one of Sammy's bedsheets that she brought so his bed here would feel more like home. She sets the Shabbat candles up on the counter between the toaster and the waffle maker.

Maria pops her head in the room to say goodbye. She has her own little room here at the motel, kind of hidden behind the office, with a bed and a desk and a dresser, but tonight she said she's going to stay at a friend's.

I hope that Mom invites her to dinner. Having company is a big part of Shabbat, probably my favorite part.

She doesn't.

"*Adios*, Maria!" I say.

Maria is teaching me three words a day. Today's words were *cama*, which means bed, *mesa*, which means table, and *motel*, which means motel. I thought that one shouldn't count because it's the same word in English, but Maria said it was still important to know that, and besides, it's not pronounced exactly the same way.

"*Hasta mañana*," says Maria. "See you tomorrow." After a few seconds I hear the tinkle of the bell as she goes out the door.

Uncle Mordy did bring barbecued chicken, plus potato kugel and couscous, along with the challahs and grape juice. I made a salad with the lettuce, cucumbers and tomatoes Mom brought back from the grocery store. Dad heats the food up in the half-size oven in the kitchen while I set the table with paper plates and plastic forks and knives. Our nice dishes are still in boxes, and Uncle Mordy won't use the plates the old owners left because they aren't from a kosher kitchen. Even Sammy helps, bringing the salt and pepper shakers from the kitchen, leaving a trail of salt behind him, like in Hansel and Gretel.

I stand next to Mom while she lights the Shabbat candles. She covers her eyes and says the blessing, then kisses me on the head and says, just loud enough for me to hear, "*Shabbat shalom*, sweetie. You've been a great sport this week and I haven't said thank you enough."

Shabbat is like that. No matter how busy the week has been, how much everyone has rushed around not having time for anything but work, on Friday night everyone takes a big breath and sees each other again.

We walk back to the table holding hands. I squeeze hers three times and she squeezes four times back for "I love you too."

This is the Mom I remember from before all this motel mess.

Everyone takes their seat at the table. Because Uncle Mordy is here, Dad does the blessings over the grape juice and challah. At home, we just eat.

Even though we're all Jewish, everyone in my family is Jewish in a different way. Especially when

45

it comes to food. My parents will eat just about anything except pork and shellfish — things like shrimp and crab and lobster — because those are the big no-nos in Judaism. Uncle Mordy, even though he's dad's brother, only eats kosher food on kosher plates, like Bubbie and Zaydie do, so no pork or shellfish for him. He also doesn't eat milk products and meat together — so no cheeseburgers. That's another big no-no if you're kosher. And he doesn't eat in restaurants unless they're kosher ones.

Dad says there's no right way and no wrong way to be Jewish. But if that's true, then why do Bubbie and Zaydie get upset when Dad takes me and Sammy to Burger King? And why did we have kosher plates back at home but eat on Mrs. Whitley's plates at the diner?

The whole thing would make a lot more sense if someone would just tell me the real rules.

It's weird, eating Shabbat dinner surrounded by cereal dispensers and labeled juice machines. Sammy's in a high chair next to me and I cut up his chicken. I can't go fast enough for him and he keeps yelling, "Mo! Mo!"

"Let me take over, squirt," says Uncle Mordy, reaching over to take Sammy's plate.

"Mi-wam do it!" Sammy says. I'm his favorite person in the world, which is both extremely cool and extremely annoying.

I ignore him this time and pick up a chicken leg, sinking my teeth into the crispy skin. I close my eyes and pretend we're back at home, eating Shabbat dinner on the special Friday night china, on top of a real tablecloth, the one that Mom's grandma made, with hundreds of tiny flowers that she embroidered herself around the edge. I picture Dahlia at her grandparents' dining-room table, listening to her father sing the blessings and fighting with her brothers over the biggest piece of challah.

"Guess what, Miriam?" Mom says. "Myrna came over this morning to introduce herself and told me you and Kate will be in the same class in September."

I open my eyes and I'm back at the Jewel, staring at a paper plate and a tablecloth with smiling red, blue and green trains on it.

I don't want to talk about school. Not when the summer just started. And not when going back to school will mean being the new kid.

"I'd think that living in a motel would make a kid seem pretty cool," says Dad, winking at me. "Wouldn't you, Mord?"

"Cool indeed."

Yeah, right. Maybe if the kid lived in the Plaza, with a doorman that greets you when you arrive and a butler on every floor. Where the faucets are real gold and a glass of OJ costs twelve dollars but doesn't taste like rust.

I figure this would be a good time to tell Mom and Dad about my grape-peeling job. I explain about the pies and tourist season and how Mrs. Whitley makes extra pies on Saturdays to prepare for all the people who come to the diner after church on Sunday.

"Sounds like fun, but not tomorrow," Mom says. "There's still tons to do around here."

"Speaking of tomorrow, Danny," says Uncle Mordy, looking at Dad. "Where is the nearest synagogue here?"

"There's one in Spartanburg, but it's twenty minutes from here."

"That's not so bad," Uncle Mordy says.

"Twenty minutes by *car*, he means," says Mom.

"How long would it take to walk?" I ask.

Uncle Mordy doesn't use a car or electricity on Friday nights or all day Saturday until the sun goes down and Shabbat is over, so he walks to his synagogue in the city. But that one is only a few blocks from his apartment.

"A long time," says Dad. "I don't think Uncle Mordy will be going to shul on Shabbat while he's here."

Shul means synagogue. And too far away is just fine with me.

5

It's Sunday. We open tomorrow.

Dad is yelling bad words at the computer at the Reception desk. Mom is shouting at Sammy, who doesn't want to put on his clothes. When I told her I was going over to the diner, she shouted at me too, handed me a broom and told me to sweep the upstairs balcony and the walkway in front of the first-floor rooms.

Shabbat is definitely over.

Only Maria is calm. She glides from one place to another, handing Mom the key she's looking for or typing something into the computer to find the file Dad needs. She even gets Sammy into his pants by pretending to put them on herself first.

In between helping everyone, she unpacks a box of brand-new bedspreads and I help her put them on the beds. They look great, except they make the carpet in the rooms look even worse.

No time for any new Spanish words.

The bakery man delivers packages of English muffins and bagels and I put them in the cabinets in the dining room. The fridge — the extra-big one for the motel — is stocked with cartons of waffle batter and gallons of milk.

Sammy gets passed around like a hot potato. Uncle Mordy has him now but asks me to take over while he goes to the hardware store in town.

I beg to go with him.

No one's taken me anywhere and I'm not allowed to go off the motel grounds on my own, except to go to the gas station down the street to buy a popsicle. The strap on my sandal broke the day after we got here and Mom promised me she'd take me to get another pair. After three days I gave up and fixed it with duct tape that I found in a drawer in Reception.

Uncle Mordy says taking Sammy would slow him down too much. Teamwork, he tells me. My family's favorite word these days.

Sammy pulls me toward the swings. The sun is hot on my neck. Mom's so busy she didn't even nag me about sunscreen. At least Sammy has a hat on. When I get tired and sweaty from pushing him and stop to give my arms a break, he starts yelling. I yell back and he starts to cry.

I wish he were older and I could talk to him. I'd tell him how much I want this whole motel thing to fail so we can go home, but because we don't have a home to go back to, it really has to work out. Maybe he would say something back that would make me feel better.

Instead, the smell of dirty diaper fills the air.

I want to be on Mrs. Whitley's team.

Around one o'clock, cars start to pull into the diner. Kate comes over and asks if I can come for lunch. Sammy's ready for his nap so Mom actually says yes. I give her a big hug to say thank you. Uncle Mordy sends me over with the leftover challah.

The diner smells amazing when we walk in, and it's not from grape pie.

"Wow," I say. "What's Mr. Whitley cooking?"

"That's the bacon," says Mrs. Whitley.

Bacon is pork, so I've never eaten it. And smelling

it makes you really want to eat it.

Most of the tables are filled with people, eating and drinking coffee and talking. Some are dressed up in pretty skirts and button-down shirts with a tie but some are wearing jeans, which is weird to me. People definitely don't wear jeans to synagogue back home.

Kate introduces me to her parents, who are sitting with another couple at a booth, and then leads me over to a little table in the corner, away from the windows.

"This is my special table," she says. "No one ever wants to sit in the corner, so Grandma says it doesn't take up a table from a real customer."

Mrs. Whitley takes the challah into the kitchen and fifteen minutes later Mr. Whitley comes out with two plates of grilled cheese sandwiches balanced on one arm and a plate piled with bacon strips on another.

The smell makes me lick my lips.

"Dig in, girls," he says, putting the plates down on the table.

"Thanks, Grandpa," says Kate. She grabs a strip of bacon and crunches off a bite. She pushes the plate toward me.

"No thanks," I say. I pick up my grilled cheese instead. It's a perfect golden brown color and the cheese is oozing out around the curves of the challah.

"How can you not want bacon?"

I start to tell her that bacon isn't kosher, but then I remember her surprise when Mom told her we don't go to church because we're Jewish.

"I'm a vegetarian," I say.

"Really? The only other vegetarian I know is my brother's girlfriend. She eats fake hot dogs that taste like cardboard, and if she sees a spider in the house, she carries it to the backyard instead of squishing it." She crunches on another piece. "I can't imagine not eating meat. I could never give up bacon."

Lekha is a vegetarian, sort of. Her parents are Hindu and believe that animals are sacred. The first time Lekha came to our house for Shabbat dinner, I forgot to tell Mom that she didn't eat animals, but when Mom passed her the plate of roast chicken she took a big piece and ate it in like three bites. She even asked for seconds! Later she told me it looked so good that she just couldn't help herself, and she made me promise not to tell her mother.

Now I know just how she felt.

Mrs. Whitley comes over with two glasses of water.

"You're right about the challah bread, Miriam. Mr. Whitley just made me the best grilled cheese sandwich I've eaten in our forty-two-year marriage."

She says challah with a regular *ch* sound in front, not the sound in Hebrew that makes it sound like you're clearing your throat.

"What do you think about the bacon?" she asks. "It's a new double-smoked kind Mr. Whitley's trying out. Made a couple of miles from here."

"Miriam's a vegetarian, Grandma," Kate says.

"Oops, sorry! Well, good for you, Miriam. I've always admired people who take a stand like that."

I feel my face burn.

"Oh, it's Father Donovan!" says Kate, waving to a man wearing a dark suit and a white collar.

"This is Miriam, Father Donovan."

"Nice to meet you." He holds out his hand and I shake it.

"Father Donovan's the priest down at the church," Mrs. Whitley tells me. "He's also one of my best customers."

"Yep," Father Donovan says, rubbing his stomach. "Especially this time of year. Myrna's grape pie is a slice of heaven here on earth."

"Miriam is Jewish," says Kate. "That's why she wasn't at church this morning."

My face burns even hotter. Why did she have to say that?

"Everyone is welcome in Greenvale," says Father Donovan. "And we're so happy to have you and your family here, Miriam. It'll be great to get the motel back in business again."

He goes to sit at the next table over just as Mom comes in.

"Oh, hi, Deborah," Mrs. Whitley says. "How are things coming along over there? You must be exhausted."

"Totally," Mom says to Mrs. Whitley. "The work never ends."

She sees the bacon on the table and raises her eyebrows at me.

"Don't worry. I didn't have any," I say.

"Miriam told us about being a vegetarian," Mrs. Whitley says. "You'll have to share some of your recipes with me."

Mom's eyebrows go even higher but she doesn't rat me out.

"Have you finished lunch? Sammy's up and I need you," she says.

"But I just got here!" I know I'm kind of whining but I can't help it. "I really want to stay and help Mrs. Whitley with the grapes."

I can tell she feels bad but she still shakes her head. "Sorry, Miriam. We open tomorrow and there's still a ton to do."

"Don't worry," Mrs. Whitley says to me. "The grapes will be here tomorrow, and the next day, and the next."

"Fine," I grumble, grabbing the rest of my sandwich.

Mom pulls a few bills out of her pocket but Mrs. Whitley waves them away. "Miriam brought over that delicious challah. That's payment enough."

Mom doesn't look happy about it but puts the money away.

I stop on the way out. "Father Donovan, this is my mom."

He stands and puts his hand out. "Wonderful to meet you. It's nice to have some new faces in town."

"Thank you, Mr. Donovan."

"It's Father Donovan," I say.

"Father Donovan," Mom says after a pause. "I'm sorry to interrupt, but I really need Miriam back at the motel."

"Of course," he says. "Please let me know if there's any way I can help."

"Bye, Kate. And thanks for lunch," I say to Mrs. Whitley, and we're out the door.

Teamwork.

The next morning, Dad replaces the Closed sign with a new one that says We're Open! Under New Management! A wooden sign that says Vacancy hangs underneath the Jewel's sign. There's a way to slide a piece of plastic back and forth to make it say No Vacancy. I weeded underneath the sign yesterday but it still looks like my dad before he's had his morning coffee.

I'm not sure how people will see the sign anyway. No one drives by here unless they're coming to the diner or getting off the highway to get gas down the street.

Check-in isn't until three o'clock though, which is hours away.

"Can I please go over and help Mrs. Whitley with the pies?" I ask Dad.

"Sure," says Dad. "I think you've earned it."

I run right over before he can change his mind or check with Mom.

Today the diner's almost empty, except for one table where a woman is drinking a cup of coffee and reading a newspaper. But even empty, it feels bright and happy, the opposite of the Jewel.

"Yoo-hoo!" I call, just like Mrs. Whitley does.

"Perfect timing, Miriam," she says as she comes out. "Just come wash your hands in the back."

I follow her back through the swinging door into the kitchen. Big pots and frying pans are piled on the metal counters, and oversized ladles and strainers hang from hooks on the walls. There are shelves on one side, some stacked with white dishes and others filled with bottles of oil and packets of flour and huge cans of tomatoes.

On one of the counters is a huge bowl of wet and shiny purple grapes. Mrs. Whitley shows me how to take a grape between my thumb and first two fingers with the part where it was attached to the stem sticking out, and gently squeeze it.

Pop! The purple skin splits and the slimy yellow-green inside pops out like a zombie eyeball, right into an empty bowl. The skins go into another bowl. No knife or peeler needed. It's way easier than I thought.

We work until all the grapes are popped and my fingertips are numb. Mrs. Whitley shows me how she cooks the peeled grapes in a pot on the stove and then strains out the seeds. Then she mixes the skins back in with the grapes. When they cool a little, she adds sugar to make the filling. I hold the bowl while she scoops it into six pie crusts that she made before I came over.

I'm not sure who is going to eat six whole pies. The woman with the newspaper left a while ago and other than some other guy coming in for two coffees to go, there haven't been any other customers.

I guess the motel being closed hasn't been good for the Whitleys either.

"Business has been slow around here with all the problems at the motel," says Mr. Whitley, like he read my mind. "But now that you're here, we're all feeling optimistic."

"What problems?" I ask him.

"Oh, don't bother her with all that, Phil. Anyway,

at the end of the summer there's a big grape festival over in Naples and lots of people will come to buy pies."

The pies are in the oven but I don't want to go back to the Jewel if someone is just going to put me to work. Working here is like being on vacation compared to the Jewel.

Mrs. Whitley has me wipe off the salt and pepper shakers on the tables with a damp cloth. I keep an eye on the motel parking lot while I work.

Around two o'clock a car pulls in.

A guest! I almost drop the pepper shaker I'm holding.

The car is kind of old looking. The words Just Married are painted in white on the rear windshield and there's a giant white ribbon tied in a bow on the antenna.

Just Married!

"Go on over," says Mrs. Whitley when she sees it. "I can't compete with that."

I pull out the money that Mom gave me for lunch but Mrs. Whitley shoos it away, then reaches into her apron pocket and hands me a crisp five-dollar bill.

"That plus lunch is more than fair for the work you put in today, Miriam."

Five dollars! I'd have popped grapes for free, just to get away from the motel for a while.

"Thank you!" I yell, running out the door.

I get to Reception right behind the man and woman. They're both wearing ripped jeans and matching T-shirts. No wedding dress. No tuxedo. Not even a bouquet of flowers.

Sammy must be taking a really long nap because Mom is alone behind the counter.

The two of them look around Reception and the man sighs.

"Do you have a room for tonight?" he asks.

Mom taps at the computer keyboard. "Yes," she says, "it looks like we have one available."

"They're all —" I start to say but Mom cuts me off.

"How many nights?"

"Just one," says the woman firmly. "We're heading to Niagara Falls for our honeymoon but we're just too tired to keep driving today."

"That'll be 55.95 plus tax for the night, with complimentary breakfast," Mom tells her.

She digs into her pocket and pulls out a neon-orange wallet. Our first paying customer!

"Since it's a special occasion," Mom says, "we'll upgrade you to a bigger room, no charge." She hands them a key card. "Room 115, up the stairs outside and to the right."

One room filled. And it's not even check-in time yet.

Maria walks in as the couple goes back out to the parking lot.

"Your first *huéspedes*!" she says. *"Felicidades!"*

Our first guests. I add *huéspedes* and *felicidades*, which Maria says means congratulations, just like *Mazel Tov*, to my mental list.

"What about bride and groom?" I ask, even though that makes four words.

"Novia y novio," Maria says. I'm going to need a notebook pretty soon.

Through the glass door, I watch the couple take a suitcase out of their trunk. I stare at the woman's jeans and flip-flops.

A real bride in a sparkly white dress with a long train and a veil down to the floor would really help brighten things up around here.

6

The voice comes from under the laundry sink.

"Do you know where your dad is?"

Uncle Mordy's legs stick out from underneath the sink. His shoes are off and he's wearing the goofy pink flamingo socks that a student gave him. He's on his back, trying to fix a leak in the pipe that connects the washing machine to the faucet. Sammy's sitting a few feet away, playing with a set of toy wrenches, banging on a bucket lying on its side.

It's really hot in here and I feel beads of sweat trickle down my nose.

"He's in the storeroom, counting. Want me to get him?"

"Never mind." Uncle Mordy grunts and lifts up his head. His face is dripping. "Hand me that hammer, would you?"

It's been a whole week since we opened. The bride and groom are long gone. There was a teenager and his mother who were on a trip to look at colleges and stayed one night. And yesterday a tow truck pulled in a fancy yellow convertible that Uncle Mordy says costs twice what a teacher makes in a whole year. It broke down right outside of Greenvale and the man said he's stuck here until the part he needs comes in, which could take two days. I'm hoping it takes longer.

You don't need a degree in hotel management to know that things are not going well.

"Uncle Mordy," I ask, "what does cooked the books mean?"

Uncle Mordy scoots out from under the sink. He grabs a rag from the toolbox and wipes his forehead.

"Where did you hear that?"

"I heard you and Dad talking about it last night. That the old owner cooked the books and that the place is practically bankrupt." I don't tell him how it scared me to hear the worry in Dad's voice.

He sighs.

"I know I shouldn't have been listening. But what does it mean?"

"It means the old owners faked the numbers in the accounts so the motel looked like it was making more money. They lied, to make the motel look like a better investment than it actually was."

That doesn't sound good.

"Hey, squirt," says Uncle Mordy, frowning back at me. "Your mom and dad are working really hard to fix this mess. Me too. We'll get the place fixed up and do some advertising on the highway."

Last week, all I wanted was for this whole thing to fail and to go home. But hearing the worry in Dad's voice and the hope in Mr. and Mrs. Whitley's, now I'm not so sure.

"But what if it doesn't work? What if we go bankrupt? Where will we live?"

"It'll be okay, Miriam. Have a little faith in the power of hard work."

I stare at my duct-taped sandal and think about how hard everyone's worked since we got here, how little time anyone's had for fun or anything else.

"But what if hard work isn't enough?"

Uncle Mordy takes a bottle of water sitting next

66

to the toolbox and pours half of it over his head. Sammy giggles.

"Then we'll just need a miracle."

"Really?" says Kate. "Where would you go?"

We're walking down to the gas station to get popsicles, staying under the trees which are the only shade around. Kate's been coming over after camp most days. She says she spends all day with her other friends and it's fun to be with someone new for a change.

I told her about the fight my parents had last night, the one I could hear right through the wall between our rooms. Someone needs to tell them that old motels don't have good soundproofing.

"That's the thing. Dad said the only option is to move in with Bubbie and Zaydie in New Jersey and Mom said no way and then Dad said that if she doesn't want to move in with his parents then they have to find a way to get people to stay in the motel."

"Bubbie and Zaydie?"

"My grandparents, on my dad's side. It's Yiddish."

"Yiddish?"

"It's an old language that the Jews used to speak in Europe. It's part German, part Hebrew."

"Cool. Do you speak it?"

"No. But my dad taught me some Yiddish insults."

"Awesome. Teach me one?"

I think, trying to remember a good one.

"*Shmendrik*. It means fool."

"*Shmendrik*," Kate repeats. It's funny hearing Yiddish come out of her mouth. "I'll have to remember that the next time my brother is being a jerk."

We squeeze around the old gas pumps and stand over the freezer case that sits right outside the door to the little store where people pay for gas, since the pumps are so ancient they don't even take credit cards.

White wisps of coolness cover us as we open the sliding door. Kate chooses a red, white and blue rocket-shaped popsicle and I grab an ice cream sandwich, even though I know it's so hot that the ice cream will ooze out the sides with every bite.

"Well, a lot of people come in for the Grape Festival at the beginning of September," Kate says as we pay inside. "Even though it's in Naples, people still come through Greenvale. The diner gets really busy and Grandma and Grandpa work until midnight some nights."

"But that's like six weeks away."

"Yeah."

We head back. There's laundry hanging on a clothesline outside one of the houses — not just shirts and jeans but also underwear. I try to imagine doing that in the city. Your clothes would get dirtier drying than they were before you washed them, with all the pollution in Manhattan.

"My mom said that the diner isn't making a profit now either, because of the motel. She wants Grandma and Grandpa to retire," Kate says.

"Wow. I can't imagine that. They both seem to love working there."

"I know. Grandma told me that if she didn't have the diner and her grape pies, she'd climb the walls with boredom. She doesn't want to sit at home or travel. She said she just wants to have a place where people can sit and talk to one another and smile when they put something sweet in their mouths."

If the Whitleys retired, then Kate wouldn't be over here practically every day.

Now there are even more reasons for the motel not to go bankrupt.

We stop under a tree for shade. A line of ants is heading somewhere. I lick the stream of white traveling down my arm.

"What if we made a better sign?" I ask, popping the last bite in my mouth. "Like repaint it or something. It's pretty pathetic, and Mom and Dad don't have time. Everyone's busy enough with the inside of the motel. Yesterday Mom was scrubbing mildew off all the shower curtains because she says there's no money to buy new ones."

"Oooh!" says Kate. "Grandpa's got a stack of paint cans in the basement. Maybe he'd let us use them. And there's a set of stencils somewhere too, from when they repainted the letters on the diner window a couple of years ago."

Kate bites off the last bit of red ice from her popsicle stick and tosses it in the garbage can on the corner.

"Last one to the diner is it!" she yells, already taking off.

I race off after her. It feels good to have a plan.

We tumble into the diner, laughing and sweating. The air conditioner is blasting and it feels like walking into a giant refrigerator.

"There you are," says Mrs. Whitley to Kate.

"Your mom will be here in ten minutes to take you to the dentist. Cleaning time."

"Oh, shoot," says Kate. "Totally forgot about that." She sticks out her tongue, which is dark purple from the popsicle.

Mrs. Whitley shakes her head. "Dr. Stevenson will love that. Let me call your mom and tell her to bring your toothbrush."

"But we were going to paint the Jewel's sign! Can we use the cans of paint in the basement? And the stencils?" asks Kate.

"I'll ask your grandfather. But after the dentist," Mrs. Whitley says.

She turns to me. "While she's there, Miriam, I'd love some help with another batch of grapes if your mom can spare you. Big church dinner this Thursday night and I'm in charge of dessert."

The bell jingles and Kate's mom comes in.

"Oops," says Mrs. Whitley. "I guess it's too late for the toothbrush."

Kate sticks her tongue out at her mother, who shakes her head exactly the way Mrs. Whitley did. "Go and rinse your mouth out at least."

She turns to me as Kate heads to the bathroom. "Hi, Miriam. How are things going next door?"

I shrug. "Not too good, really. But Kate and I are going to paint the sign, make it look new."

"Sounds like a good idea. I'll have her back in about an hour."

I run over to the Jewel after they leave to ask Mom about the grapes.

"Sure," she says, surprising me. "Just take Sammy along, would you, honey?" Sammy looks up from the floor where he's making towers of blocks.

"Seriously? You know he'll just get in the way."

Her eyebrows go up.

"For real, Mom. It's just an hour."

"Miriam —"

"I know, I know," I grumble, giving her my own eyes of death and holding my hand out to my brother. "Family first."

"So, what's our color scheme?" Kate asks, looking down from the stepladder.

At my feet are a bunch of open paint cans and a stack of brushes that Mr. Whitley gave us. I stir the white paint around, lift out the mixing stick and watch it drip down like maple syrup onto a pancake. There are also a couple of smaller cans in different colors. One is called Sapphire Blue.

72

We've sanded off the flaking yellowy paint like Mr. Whitley showed us. Sammy's already sticky and purple from eating cut-up grapes at the diner but I strip off his T-shirt and shorts and let him toddle around in his diaper.

"Sapphire is a kind of jewel, right?" I ask. "How about we do the post and the background white, and then do the lettering in blue, with a black outline?" I say.

Sammy wants to help, of course, so I give him a paintbrush and a cup of water and let him "paint" the bottom of the post, the only part he can reach. I hope he doesn't stomp on the pink and white petunias Mom planted around the base. He's so happy it makes me laugh.

It takes two coats of white before the old letters no longer show through. We swing on the swings and wait for it to dry, while Sammy digs in the sandbox.

A car pulls up next to us in the parking lot, with Georgia license plates. Woo-hoo!

A woman sticks her head out the window.

"I'm looking for the Daisy Inn in Spartanburg?"

Kate shakes her head. "This is Greenvale. Spartanburg is the next exit."

73

The woman drives off.

"What's in Spartanburg?"

"The university. The motels there get tons of business at the end of the summer, with all the parents coming to drop off their kids for the school year."

She jumps off the swing and turns around to face me.

"The problem with Greenvale is that we don't have anything people come to see. Not even a museum or a racetrack. It's just some place people come through on their way to somewhere else."

"My dad says there's a synagogue in Spartanburg. Not that that would attract tourists."

"How come you don't go there every week, like we go to church?"

I shrug. "We used to when I was little and we lived near Bubbie and Zaydie. But when we moved to the city, we stopped."

We check on the sign. It's dry enough so we use the stencils to outline the letters and then paint them in while Sammy paints his post again.

It's gotten pretty hot and the petunias look wilted. Kate finds a bucket and we fill it with water and drag it back together to water everything.

We step back to get a good look.

"It looks great," says Kate.

And it does.

After we put the paint away, Kate bikes home. Sammy needs a bath but I'm starving so I take him through Reception on the way to the dining room. Mom's on the phone but points to a pile of mail on the counter. On top there's a postcard addressed to me.

"Greetings from Camp Maplewood!" the front says, under a photo of kids in a canoe. On the back it says, *Camp is awesome. I can waterski now! How is the motel? I hope there will be a room left for me to stay in when I come visit you. I miss you!!!! Love, Lekha.* She's drawn little hearts around the edges.

A room left? More like ten.

I grab a bagel and an apple that's not too bruised and take the postcard back to Room 109 and lie on the bed, watching a fly buzz around the light fixture. If it's not careful, it'll end up joining the collection of dead ones inside.

When Dahlia's back from Israel and Lekha's back from camp, the plan is for both of them to come up to visit the weekend before school starts. Mom said she'd have Sammy sleep in her room and bring a cot into Room 109 so the three of us can have a sleepover just like we used to back home.

I look out my window at the empty parking lot. New York City feels like a million miles away.

7

I have nothing to do the next day. Kate's at camp and the motel is empty, except for one guy on his way back home to somewhere in Canada who is leaving this morning if he ever wakes up.

Even Maria has time for a cup of coffee on the balcony.

There's no one around to notice the sign got a new paint job.

In the storeroom I find a carton of brownie mix that's almost expired and let Sammy help me make them. By the time we get them in the oven, he's covered with chocolate. He looks like he ran through a mud puddle.

"Want a bath, Samster?"

"Toys!" he says. Sammy could spend all day in the tub with his bath toys. And at least it's something to do while we wait for the brownies to cook.

I take the timer so I'll know when they're done and we head downstairs.

I hear Maria singing in Spanish in Room 106 while she changes the sheets. The Canada guy must have finally left.

"Hola, Miri," she says, using her nickname for me.

"Hola, Maria," I say back, trying to copy her accent.

Sammy reaches for the squishy ball on the keychain hanging from the cleaning cart and squeals when it lights up. I grab a pillow and pull off the case to help out. Sunlight hits Maria's necklace, making it sparkle. I can't stop looking at it.

"Want to try it on?" she asks.

"Can I?"

Maria clasps the necklace around my neck and I look at myself in the mirror, twisting back and forth, the color of the cross changing as I move.

"It's made of opal," Maria says. "My grandmother gave it to me for my confirmation."

"What's a confirmation?"

"It's a ceremony you do when you are old enough to understand what it means to be a Catholic."

I look at her reflection behind me in the mirror. It sounds kind of like a bar mitzvah. Dahlia's older brother David had his last year. He read from the Torah in front of the whole congregation and made a speech and after there was a fancy lunch at the synagogue to celebrate. Bubbie's been asking Mom and Dad when my bat mitzvah will be, but they never seem to answer. I'm not even sure if I want one.

"How do you say grandmother in Spanish?" I ask.

"*Abuela*. And grandfather is *abuelo*."

"*Abuela*," I repeat. I have a necklace from my grandmother too, that she gave me when I was born. It's a little hand about the size of a dime, but the thumb and the pinky are the same size. It's called a hamsa in Hebrew, which means five, because of the five fingers. It's supposed to be good luck. It's in my jewelry box in my dresser since I feel funny wearing it here. Kate might think it's weird.

And it doesn't sparkle like Maria's cross.

"It's beautiful." I twist back and forth some more and it seems to wink at me. "Do you ever take it off?" I can't remember seeing her without it since we got here.

"Almost never. Abuela has the same one. It helps me feel closer to her when she's so far away."

"Where does she live?"

"She's back in Mexico. I miss her tons." Maria sighs and lifts my hair to undo the clasp.

"How do you say necklace in Span —"

Sammy gasps and we turn to see him sitting under a pile of little shampoo bottles that used to be in a box on Maria's cart. One of them must have been open because there's shampoo dripping down his head. We laugh but that makes him cry.

"Looks like you got a head start on that bath," I tell him, picking him up and kissing his nose just as the timer goes off. "Let's get the brownies out of the oven and then — bath time!"

The water is draining from the tub and Sammy's still playing with his bath toys when Mom comes in.

"Hi, Mom. I made brownies, did you see?"

She bends down to give me a kiss on top of my head.

"What's that around your neck?"

I reach up and feel the necklace. "Oh, it's Maria's. I was trying it on and then Sammy spilled the shampoo and —"

"Take it off, please."

I look in the mirror and take the cross in my fingers. "It was her grandmother's. Isn't it pretty? When the sun shines on it —"

"I said, take it off."

I turn to her. "Maria said I could try it on," I say. "Don't be mad."

"I'm not mad," she says, but her voice is tight.

I fumble with the clasp until Mom spins me around and unclasps it herself. I catch it before it hits the counter top.

"You're Jewish, Miriam. Jews don't wear crosses."

"It's just a necklace, Mom."

"It is *not* just a necklace, Miriam. It's a cross. And people have done hateful things to Jews in the name of that cross. Don't you ever forget that. Okay?" She's raising her voice and Sammy looks up at her, and then me, and starts to cry.

Where the heck did that come from? My hand makes a fist around the cross and the edges bite into my hand.

"Okay?" she repeats. Her hands are shaking a little and she's looking past me at nothing I can see.

"Okay," I say, my eyes hot, and rush out of the room, slamming the door on my way out.

I run across the parking lot, ignoring the gravel that gets in my sandals. The annoying bell ting-a-lings but thankfully the office is empty. I stop at the closed door to Maria's room behind the front desk. No one answers when I knock, and I hesitate only a second before trying the door.

It swings open.

The room is pretty bare — just a bed, a desk and a dresser covered with framed photos. There's one of Maria and some other people in front of a waterfall. Another photo must be her with her brother and sister, because they look just like her, with dark hair and wide smiles.

I've never asked her about her family. I see one of her and an older woman who must be her *abuela*. She's wearing a cross like Maria's.

I carefully put the necklace on the dresser and turn to go. There's a pile of papers on the desk and I know I shouldn't, but I take a look. There's a booklet with Upstate University School of Medicine printed on the cover, filled with photos of smiling students wearing white coats, bending over smiling patients.

Maria wants to go to medical school? Then why is she working cleaning rooms at a motel?

Underneath is an application of some sort, partly filled out in Maria's neat writing. But it's not an application to medical school.

It's an application for a job at a coffee shop. In Spartanburg.

The phone at the front desk rings while I stare at the job application.

Maria wants to leave? She never said anything about that to me. Doesn't she know we need her here? That *I* need her here?

The phone is still ringing. I gather the papers back into a pile and go out, closing the door behind me. I get to the phone just in time to say, "Jewel Motor Inn" to a dial tone.

Whatever. Let them stay someplace else. This place is a hopeless disaster anyway.

I stomp out of the office toward my room and there, right in front of it, is the person I least want to see right now. I push past her, catching my elbow on the sharp edge of the cleaning cart.

"Darn it!" I look down at the blood already starting to drip from the deep scratch.

"Ay!" says Maria, grabbing a tissue off the cart. "Let me take a look at that."

I pull away from her. "It's fine."

83

"Hold on, I have a Band-Aid here somewhere." She rummages through a box on top of the cart.

"It's fine," I say again. "Just leave me alone." I fumble to get the keycard off my wrist so I can get into my room before the tears come.

Maria steps in front of me, a worried look on her face.

"What is it, Miri? What happened?"

"Nothing," I lie. "What do you care anyway? You're just going to leave and get another job at some dumb coffee shop."

I get around her and let the door slam behind me and throw myself onto my hard-as-a-rock, squeaky bed.

I'm mad. Mad at Mom for being so mean about the necklace and at Maria for leaving and Dahlia and Lekha for being far away while I'm stuck in this disgusting place that I'm supposed to call home.

I ignore Maria calling at me to open the door until she gives up.

Mom comes in with Sammy to put him down for his nap. She leans over me and whispers, "Sorry I got upset, sweetie. I love you, you know."

I pretend to be asleep. She strokes my hair a few times, turns on the baby monitor and goes out.

When I'm sure she's gone I get up quietly so I don't wake my brother and slip out of the room.

I'm sitting alone in the dining room eating my third brownie when Maria comes in and sits down across from me. I stare at my plate.

"Those smell great," she says. "Enough for me?"

I push the pan over to her without saying anything.

"You were in my room," she says.

I don't answer.

"It's okay, I'm not mad. Thank you for returning my necklace." I glance up and see it's around her neck again.

I shrug.

"I'm guessing you saw the application," she says.

I nod.

"When I left Mexico to come to the US, I planned to go to college and then medical school. The nearest doctor to my village is two hours away. It's been my dream to go back there as a doctor, to help the people I grew up with. I figured I'd be here eight years, tops."

I don't look at her but I'm listening.

"Things didn't go exactly the way I planned. My boyfriend from back home had already come here

85

to go to Spartanburg U, where he got a scholarship. I applied and got a scholarship too, but then we broke up and I needed a place to live. I ran out of money pretty quickly. I got some loans and a job on campus and finished my college degree, but then I realized I would need to take some time off after graduation to make some money before I could go to medical school."

"Working here pays better than the other jobs I found. Not a lot better, but better. It's steady work, not shifts here and there like coffee shops or grocery stores, and it comes with a free place to live, so I can save even more money. But, well, you know. The motel hasn't been doing so well for a while. When your family bought the place I had more hope. I still do, but if the motel closes, I have to have another job to go to. I've worked really hard to get to this point and I'm not willing to give up my dream. Can you understand that?"

I feel ashamed that I never thought of Maria as having a whole other life and not just being here to clean the rooms and be my friend. It can't be fun cleaning toilets and changing dirty sheets all day.

"Yeah," I whisper. "But that doesn't mean I want you to go."

She smiles. "I know. We can hope and pray that things turn around. I see that you and Kate painted the sign. It looks great."

We eat our brownies together. She gives me a hug and grabs another brownie on her way out. *"Riquísimo, gracias."*

I turn around to look through the window down at the sign. It does look great.

I just hope it will be enough. Now Kate and I need to save the motel *and* the diner *and* Maria's job.

This calls for a fourth brownie.

8

Painting the sign was a total fail. I think we've had all of three rooms booked this whole week. I'm so bored I think I'm going bananas. Mom and Dad are super cranky and Sammy and I just try to stay out of their way.

I go from empty room to empty room trying all the TVs but there's still nothing a kid who can speak in complete sentences would want to watch. I end up spending the morning in Room 112, which gets the best reception, reading one of the ancient magazines I took from the stash under the coffee table in Reception, while Sammy is mesmerized by a cartoon squirrel singing about sharing acorns so everyone has enough for the winter. Someone should tell him it's still July.

Kate was home sick the end of last week but finally comes over after church on Sunday. We play Spit on the rickety picnic table next to the playground, trying not to get splinters. I tell Kate all about Maria and her job and how now it's even more important that the motel doesn't go bankrupt.

I deal out the cards as a minivan pulls into the parking lot and a woman steps out.

"I think I got off at the wrong exit." She consults a piece of paper in her hand. "Exit 35?"

"This is Exit 33," says Kate.

"Ugh, I'm such a dope," says the woman. "And the kids need a bathroom."

I tell her she can use the one in the motel, hoping that Mom won't notice since only guests are supposed to use the bathrooms.

"Honestly," says Kate when the van drives off. "No one comes to Greenvale for anything."

"What about your grandma's pies?"

"They just come in and buy them on their way to somewhere else. They don't stay."

"There must be something here. What about those caves in the pamphlet in Reception? Don't people go to see those?"

"Those are thirty minutes away, just outside of Brookdale. Which has two motels, by the way."

"Well, there must be something else." I stop talking so I can concentrate on my cards, throwing down my last one and slapping the smaller pile.

"How do you play so fast?" Kate asks, grabbing the bigger pile.

"Practice?" I shrug. "You should see Dahlia play. I haven't beaten her in years." I deal my cards out into five piles. "But really, what else is there in this town?"

"There used to be a drive-in movie theater, but it closed like five years ago. Now there's just a big peeling screen and a parking lot full of weeds."

"So maybe we need to make something for people to come see," I say.

"Like what?"

"Like …I don't know. But there must be something."

"Go!" says Kate, catching me off guard. I catch up but my last card slips through the slots of the table to the ground underneath, giving her enough time to throw out her last card and grab the smaller pile.

"Ha!"

"Lucky break," I say.

"This is boring," Kate says.

"Sure, because you're still losing."

"Let's go for a bike ride," she says.

A bike ride? I haven't been on a bike for over a year, and that was just going up and down the paths in Central Park, not on real roads.

"Mom will never let me. And besides, I don't have a bike."

"City girl," says Kate, rolling her eyes. "How do you not have a bike?"

"Because we have this great thing called a subway," I shoot back. "Have you ever even been on one?"

"I went on the bus once, in Spartanburg."

"Country girl," I say, rolling my eyes.

For a second I think we're going to have our first fight, but then Kate does this thing with her eyes where she makes them go all white and I crack up.

"I'm pretty sure Grandma has some old bikes in her garage that she never got rid of. Let's go ask your mom," Kate says.

We find Mom at the computer. Kate tells her that all the kids bike on the roads here, that there's plenty of room on the shoulders, and that she wants to show me the town and the school.

It's like she knows exactly how to get my mom to say yes. I pay close attention.

One of the bikes at Mrs. Whitley's fits, and there's a helmet too. I'm a little wobbly at first but it comes back quickly and before I know it, I'm coasting down a long, not-too-steep hill behind Kate. The sun is warm on my face and the wind rushes past my ears.

"Let's go see the school first," Kate yells from in front of me, her voice carried on the wind.

We get to Hollingsworth Middle School in about ten minutes. The red brick building is just one story high and all sprawled out, not narrow and tall like my school back home. There's a big parking lot in front and great big soccer and baseball fields in the back. It's all so green.

Our next stop is the library, where Kate introduces me to the librarian. The building is pretty big, given how small the town is, but there's only one librarian in the whole place.

At home the library has about twenty people working behind the desk. The librarian tells me to come back with a parent and he'll sign me up for a library card.

We bike another fifteen minutes, past a huge cornfield and another field that Kate says are sunflowers, although right now they're only about knee high and the flowers haven't opened. It's mostly uphill and my legs burn to keep up with her.

I'm panting as we turn in next to the Mike's Drive-In sign at the entrance to a huge, empty parking lot. The pavement is cracked and overgrown with weeds. The lines that mark the parking spots are all faded. There are metal posts between the spots. Kate says that's where the speakers used to hang, attached to a cord so you could hook them on your car window.

"Did you ever see a movie here?" I ask.

"Nah. It closed before I was born. But my parents told me all about it. Lightning hit the projection booth and fried the sound system, or something like that."

"Wow."

"Yeah. They never reopened. I think not enough people were coming."

We bike past the abandoned concession stands, where Kate says they used to sell popcorn and candy, pedaling slowly over the cracks and bumps as we head over to the far end to the movie screen.

I crane my neck to see the whole thing. It's huge from down here.

Kate hops off her bike and I follow her. We lie down on the warm asphalt, staring up at it. She's barely broken a sweat while I'm still trying to catch my breath.

I stare at the huge screen. It's definitely not going to show a movie any time soon, with all those tears and cracks and rust stains.

"We used to play this game when we were little, me and my brother, looking for pictures in the cracks. There's a dragon in one of the corners." She studies the screen. "There!" She points. "Do you see it?""

It takes me a moment but then I see how the cracks kind of make a dragon snout with fire coming out of it.

"And there's an ice cream cone near the bottom." She waggles her finger until I see it. "I can't believe I still remember them."

"It's like constellations," I say. "How about over there?" I point to an area in the middle. "It kind of looks like a face."

"Where?"

"Right there. See where that oval rust stain is? Right underneath. It looks like a woman with long hair."

"I see it," says Kate. "The rust stain gives her a halo."

"So she must be an angel," I say.

"Or the Virgin Mary," says Kate.

"The Virgin Mary?"

"Yeah, you know, the mother of Jesus. You know who Jesus is, right?"

"Of course I know who Jesus is."

"Well, how do I know? You're Jewish, right?"

"I read an article about the Virgin Mary in one of the old magazines in Reception," I tell her. "Some people in Europe somewhere said they saw her on a hill. Near some tiny town that no one knew about. Now thousands of people go there every year. They even had to build a hotel for all the people to stay in."

I close my eyes and let the warmth from the ground seep into my sore muscles.

Kate clears her throat. I open my eyes and she's staring at me.

"Did you hear what you just said?"

I close my eyes again. "Just because I'm Jewish doesn't mean I can't read ten-year-old magazine articles about the Virgin Mary."

"What. You. Just. Said."

I sit up.

"That I'm Jewish or that I read magazines?" Seriously, what is her problem?

"Thousands of people. Hotel."

"What are you talking about?" She's starting to tick me off.

"You said thousands of people came and they had to build a *hotel*," she shouts, throwing her arms out.

Oh. My. God.

We race back home, drop the bikes behind the diner, grab the magazine I was reading and run to Room 109. We fill the ice bucket to the top and gulp down cold water and figure out a plan.

Uncle Mordy said that if hard work didn't save the motel, we'd need a miracle.

Kate and I are going to make one.

9

When I wake up the next morning there's a note under the door. I'm sure it's from Kate but when I open it, I read:

Meet me at the pool at 10:00.
Swimming lessons start today!

Love,
Your Favorite Uncle

Ha! Uncle Mordy is my only uncle. And if he thinks he's going to give me swimming lessons, he's no longer my favorite.

When I was six, I fell out of a rowboat into Turtle Lake when we were on vacation. I was wearing a life jacket but I totally panicked. My hair was plastered over my face and I couldn't see anything and seaweed got tangled around my ankle and I was sure a turtle or an eel was about to bite me.

Dad scooped me right out of the water and back into the boat, but I couldn't stop crying, and then I threw up. Now, whenever I get near a lake or a pool, my heart starts to beat out of my chest and I can't catch my breath. I know it's ridiculous but I can't help it. Even the word swimming makes my stomach ache. Mom wants to take me to therapy to help me get over it but Dad says I just need time. I'm happy to let them argue about it while I avoid water in anything but a bathtub or a cup.

"No swimming lessons," I tell Uncle Mordy at breakfast. There are so few guests that he has time to sit and eat with me. "I'm not feeling well. And besides, didn't you and Dad say you were meeting with that lawyer today in Spartanburg?"

If the plan Kate and I came up with works, they won't need to meet with any lawyer to try and get money back from the motel's old owner, but I can't tell him that.

"I will not be distracted, Miriam Brockman," he says, pointing a finger at me like I'm one of his fifth graders at school. "You have a bathing suit here, right?"

Maria pops her head into the room. *"Buenos días!* Anyone know where the extra light bulbs went? They used to be in the storeroom but now they're gone." She smiles at Uncle Mordy, then waves at me. "Light bulbs. *Bombillas.*"

"Bombillas," I repeat. "Cool word."

"Cool as a girl in a pool at the Jewel," Uncle Mordy sings.

Maria laughs even though Uncle Mordy is acting like a little kid.

"I used the last one yesterday," he says, smiling back at her. "I'll get some more this afternoon in town."

For a guy who said he will not be distracted, Uncle Mordy's looking pretty distracted to me.

He stands up and points again. "Pool. Ten o'clock." He grabs his plate and heads to the kitchen. I can hear him whistling as he loads the dishwasher.

I get to the pool a few minutes early. My heart is beating faster just being in a room with a pool, and I need to pee even though I just went before I changed into my suit. I'm starting to feel sick for real now and I'm even more sure that swimming lessons are a really bad idea.

I grab my towel and start to leave when Uncle Mordy walks in.

"No way, kid. Your mom promised me half an hour with no interruptions. Today's goal: in up to your knees."

Half an hour? Going in up to my knees couldn't take more than five minutes. I can do that.

Uncle Mordy leads me over to the side of the pool near the steps.

"No splashing," I say.

"No splashing."

"No water above the knees."

"No water above the knees." He holds my hand and I step down onto the top step. The water laps at my ankles. I try to pretend I've stepped into the bathtub and not a pool, but the water is cooler and the chlorine stinks and makes my eyes sting. I hold onto the metal handrail for dear life.

Uncle Mordy makes googly eyes at me. I can't help laughing and as I do, he takes my other hand and before I can do anything about it, I'm on the second step. The water tickles at my calves. I close my eyes and pretend that I'm in a sandbox and my feet are buried in warm sand instead of water.

"How are you doing?"

"Okay," I say, opening my eyes. This isn't so bad.

"So, I hear you're learning a little Spanish."

"Yeah. I've filled a couple of pages in my note-book already. Pool is *piscina*." I tell him the other words I remember.

It turns out that Uncle Mordy took Spanish in high school. I wonder if Maria knows that.

"One more step?" Uncle Mordy asks. "Half hour's almost up."

Really? We just started. I look up at the clock on the far wall and see that he's right.

I take a deep breath, close my eyes again and squeeze Uncle Mordy's hand like I'm trying to get toothpaste out of an empty tube. I step down to the next step.

"Hey, you did it, Mir!"

I open my eyes to check, even though I can feel the water tickling behind my knees. My toes look bigger under water. Uncle Mordy lets go of my hands and I'm standing on the third step all by my-self, up to my knees, and it's all okay. Great, even.

101

The door opens and a guest walks in. He drops his towel onto one of the pool chairs and dives into the deep end. He's not close enough to splash me but the water surges up past my knees. I'm sure I'm going to slip beneath the water and drown. My heart pounds. I race up the steps. My legs are wobbly. I grab my towel and stand a few feet away from the side of the pool and take big deep breaths.

Uncle Mordy is there in a second. He puts his hand on my shoulder while I catch my breath.

"You did it!" He's grinning like I just won the Olympics or something. "Up to your knees!"

I look down at the water dripping off my legs. I did do it! If I were home, I'd call Dahlia and Lekha but they probably wouldn't believe me. As long as they've known me, I don't do pools.

"Next time we'll go down one more step," Uncle Mordy says.

Next time?

"Let's go get you a Ring Pop to celebrate. There was a blue raspberry one in front when I walked by this morning."

It's not watermelon, but it will do.

Mom's on the phone at Reception with Sammy at her feet. She gives me a thumbs up when she sees me. We pass Dad on our way to the vending machine and I tell him about my big accomplishment.

"Strong work, Miriam!" he says, high-fiving me.

Uncle Mordy gets a Ring Pop for Sammy too. We head back to Reception, where Mom's struggling to unjam the printer. She hands Sammy over to me and doesn't even protest when Uncle Mordy gives him the candy, even though I'm pretty sure I wasn't allowed to eat a Ring Pop until I was in third grade.

"How a printer can jam printing out all of three receipts in a week is beyond me," I hear her say as I head over to the swings.

I don't even mind babysitting because after camp today Kate is meeting me at the diner to discuss our plan.

"So, this is what I figured out last night," says Kate.

We're at her table in the corner of the diner looking through some stuff she printed out from the internet.

Mrs. Whitley comes over with a couple of Cokes, and Kate slams the papers upside down.

Mrs. Whitley looks at us sideways, then shakes her head. "I'm sure I don't want to know. Just promise me it doesn't involve fire."

"I promise," Kate tells her. "No fire."

"Fire?" I ask as her grandmother walks off. "For real?"

"Jeez, I was only eight and it wasn't on purpose. And no one got hurt."

We finish reading and Kate grabs her backpack and one of the small cans of paint and we jump on the bikes and go back out to the drive-in.

It only takes a second to find the face, now that we know where to look.

"We should put the cross there, right under the face," Kate says, pointing.

It sounded like a good plan when we were back in the diner, but now the screen just looks huge and super high up, sitting on a metal frame.

We stand at the bottom and look up. From this angle you can't see the screen anymore. We walk around to the back. There's a ladder on the side and scaffolding all the way up the back.

"We could climb up the ladder," Kate says.

"Are you kidding me? That's like a hundred feet up or something. And then what? We'll be at the back. How would you get to the front to paint it?"

We stare at the screen until my neck starts to ache.

"I know," Kate says. She rummages through her backpack and comes out with a red Swiss Army knife.

"My brother's," she says. "It'll be perfect." She shoves it into her jeans pocket.

"Are you serious?"

"Just trust me," she says. "Let's go. Hope you're not afraid of heights."

I follow her up the zigzagging steps next to the screen. They remind me of the fire escapes on the outside of the buildings back home in Manhattan.

I'm not afraid of heights, exactly, but climbing up this high outside is way different from being at the top of a skyscraper on the inside.

At the bottom of the movie screen, a platform leads across to the other end of the screen. The steps continue up to the top of the screen.

I look at Kate. There's no way I'm going up any more than this. I follow her a couple of feet onto the platform. There's a railing, which I hold onto tightly.

We're behind the screen, and now that we're up here I realize just how big it is. Even if I stretch my arms up all the way, I probably don't reach even a tenth of the way to the top.

Kate pulls the knife out of her pocket. She walks back and forth a few feet.

"I think it's probably around here," she says, pointing to the back of the screen.

"What is?"

"The face. I need to put the cross under it, right?"

I'm having a hard time imagining the screen from the other side, and I'm starting to get a little freaked out. The metal platform shakes a little as Kate walks back and forth, and I grip the railing tighter.

It's not as bad as when I'm near a pool, but still, I'm ready to get back to solid earth.

"Okay," Kate says. "I'm going to do it here." She pushes the knife into the back of the screen. She needs to push pretty hard but the knife goes through. She makes a vertical cut about two or three feet long and then another shorter one, horizontally, about a foot from the top, wiggling the knife back and forth as she goes to make the cut jagged.

"Done. Let's get down," she says. She reaches behind her to put the knife in her pocket and loses her balance, grabbing for the railing. The knife drops, clattering against the metal steps as it goes down, down, down.

"Crap," says Kate, steadying herself. "My brother's going to kill me."

"It's okay," I say. "We'll find it. Let's just get off this thing."

Going down is even more freaky than going up. I grip the handrails so hard my fingers start to hurt.

Just as we reach the bottom, I hear the sound of crunching gravel.

A police car is pulling into the far end of the lot.

"Shoot," says Kate. Her eyes are practically wider than her face. "Police!"

We barrel down the last few steps and race over to our bikes just as the squad car pulls up.

An officer gets out of the car. "What are you kids doing out — oh, it's you, Kate."

Kate's face relaxes. "Oh, hi, Officer Mike." She gets back off her bike. "This is Miriam. Her parents bought the Jewel Motor Inn."

He shakes my hand. "Welcome to Greenvale."

She turns to me. "Officer Mike used to work in the diner, before he went to police officer school."

Everyone knows everyone in this town.

"What are you two doing out here, anyway?"

She shoots me a look. "I was just taking Miriam around, showing her where stuff is. We stopped here to rest."

"At this dump?" Officer Mike laughs. "There must be nicer places in Greenvale to show your friend."

"Do you think they'll ever show movies here again?" Kate asks.

"Doubt it," Officer Mike says. "Screen's a mess."

We all stare up at it.

Kate points at the left corner. "Miriam and I were trying to decide if that looks like a dragon over there. And there's definitely a lady's face where that rust stain is. It's almost like a halo."

I look at Kate with a what-the-heck expression, but she gives me a just-shut-up look back.

"Huh," he says, staring at it. He walks back a few steps, squints, then moves his head from side to side. He pulls out his phone and takes a picture of the screen.

He turns back to us. "Okay, you guys. Technically, you're trespassing, so grab your bikes and let's get you out of here."

We put on our helmets while he stares back up at the screen.

As we bike off we hear him on his walkie-talkie. "Number 34, this is Number 21. Can you pop over to the drive-in on Birch? Something I want you to see here. Over."

Two days later I'm eating breakfast with Sammy when Uncle Mordy comes in holding a copy of the *Greenvale Herald.*

"Where's your dad?"

"In the back room, counting cereal." It seems like the only thing to do around here these days is count things.

"Daniel, come take a look at this," Uncle Mordy calls.

Dad comes out and drops a box of single-serving sugar cereals on the chair next to me. At home I'm only allowed to eat sugar cereals on Shabbat morning, as a treat. Here, no one notices that I have one every day.

I read over his shoulder. The headline on the front page reads "*Is It Her? Local Officer Discovers Image of Virgin Mary at Drive-In.*"

There's a photo of the drive-in screen, zoomed in to the area where we saw the face. It's blurry and in black and white but it's there. The cross is too, kind

109

of faint, but visible. Officer Mike is quoted in the article: "I pulled into the drive-in as part of my beat — you know, just checking to make sure everything was A-okay — and I looked up and there she was, as clear as day. Just beautiful."

I hold my breath as I read, but the article doesn't mention me or Kate.

I can't believe it worked!

I scan the rest of the article, which talks about another Virgin Mary sighting in upstate New York in 1920, which apparently was declared fake by the Church.

Uncle Mordy hums as he reads but I'm freaking out.

The Church investigates Virgin Mary apparitions? Does Kate know this?

"Things are about to get interesting," Dad says. "Deborah's not going to like this."

I'm not sure why Mom wouldn't like this, but I'm caught between hope that people will come to Greenvale to see it and terror that we'll be found out.

Interesting doesn't quite capture it.

It's not even eight o'clock the next morning but Uncle Mordy's already at the Reception desk, the phone tucked under his ear while he scribbles on a pad of paper.

"Go find your father," he whispers when I walk in the door, Sammy following behind me, still in his pajamas. "The computer won't boot and —"

"Yes, we have rooms available," Uncle Mordy says into the phone in his normal voice. "How many nights?" He scribbles some more. "How many? Yeah, sure, we can do that."

He holds his hand over the mouthpiece and waves at me. "Your father, *now*."

I search for Dad, practicing my Spanish as I go. He isn't in Room (*Habitación*) 110 or the dining room (*el comedor*) or the laundry room (*la lavandería*) or the pool room (*la piscina*).

Sammy starts to whine and lag behind so I give him a piggyback to the upstairs balcony. Maria's cleaning cart is blocking the door to Room 112, where one of the two guests we had last night was staying. She hasn't seen Dad either.

I hurry back to Reception. Uncle Mordy's still on the phone. He has a calendar in front of him now and is scribbling names into the boxes. He looks up for a second and I shrug and hold my hands up. I lift Sammy onto the counter and Uncle Mordy hands him a pretzel log that he pulls out of some-where.

"Three miles south of center Greenvale off High-way 30. Exit 33," Uncle Mordy says into the phone. "Check-in is at 3:00 p.m. We'll see you tomorrow, then. Have a safe drive." He hangs up the phone and sticks out his tongue. "Whew! It's barely eight and I'm exhausted."

The phone rings again.

"Sorry," Uncle Mordy says into it after a minute. "We're full tonight and tomorrow … Sure, I can book you for Monday." He makes a few notes on the calendar.

"What do you mean, full?" I say when he hangs up.

"Full. Booked. No vacancy." He shakes his head just as Dad walks in. "Unbelievable."

I can't believe my ears. "No vacancy? Really?"

"Yep. And all thanks to the Virgin Mary," Uncle Mordy says.

Dad laughs. "That proves it."

"Proves what?" I say.

"There *is* a God."

"There certainly is," a voice says behind us.

I turn around. It's Father Donovan, smiling. I

almost didn't recognize him without his suit. Today he's wearing jeans and a Yankees cap and holding a to-go cup of coffee from the diner.

"Just the person I've been looking for," he says, pointing at me.

Can priests tell when they're looking at someone guilty, like X-ray vision?

"I …"

"Mrs. Whitley sent me. Says your phone line has been busy all morning and she can't leave the diner to come over. She wants to know if you have time this morning to help with a batch of grape pies." He rubs his stomach. "I'm hoping you do."

I breathe out again and look at Dad. "I'll take Sammy. Please?"

"Sure," he says. "Looks like we're going to get busy pretty soon but I think we can spare you for an hour or two."

I go back to Room 109 to grab some toys for Sammy and we head to the diner.

I can't wait until after camp so I can tell Kate it worked!

And wait until Mrs. Whitley hears that the motel is going to be full. We're going to need way more grape pies.

10

"Miri," says Maria. *"Como estás?* I've hardly seen you since the place got so busy."

It's been two weeks since the article about the Virgin Mary was in the *Greenvale Herald*. After that the story got picked up by the big paper out in Spartanburg and then the even bigger papers and since then the Jewel has been full every night.

Dad was actually singing in the shower this morning. I could hear him through the wall, he was so loud.

I've filled Maria's cart with clean towels and restocked the soaps and shampoos and now I'm in Room 104, waiting for her to tell me what she wants me to do next. Mom finally hired a babysitter for

Sammy, so now I help Maria in the morning, and then I'm free in the afternoon to work at the diner or bike or read and then hang out with Kate after she comes back from camp. Mrs. Whitley makes grape pies every day and still runs out by dinner time. She gives me five dollars every time I help, saying she'd never be able to keep up without me. I stick them in the back of my dresser and the pile is really growing.

"*Todo está bien?*" says Maria, looking at me. "Everything okay?"

"*Muy bien,*" I tell her, and it's true.

As she starts pulling the sheets off the bed, Maria chatters on about how busy we are and how exciting the apparition is and how now she won't have to find another job. I grab the pillows and shake them hard to get them out of their cases. She grabs a fresh bottom sheet from the cart and I help tuck the corners over the mattress on my side.

As we work, I start to worry. What will happen to all this new business if we get found out? If people find out the apparition isn't real, will they stop coming to see it?

It sounds weird even to me, since I don't believe in the Virgin Mary or in apparitions to begin with.

"Maria," I say, "what do *you* think about the drive-in?"

Maria grabs a top sheet. She flicks her wrists and the sheet floats up over the bed like a parachute and then settles down perfectly over the mattress.

"It would be wonderful if there were *un milagro* in Greenvale," Maria says. I help put new cases on the pillows as she tucks the blanket and sheets in tightly.

"Un milagro," I repeat. A miracle. The word rolls off my tongue. "But do *you* think it's a miracle?"

She shrugs. "It's a miracle that the Jewel is full, no?"

She whistles as she checks the room for anything she's forgotten, closes the door behind us, and then pushes the cart toward the next room.

"Let's go. So much work to do!"

Maria is so happy. I can't help but be happy too.

Mom hangs up the phone and holds her head in her hands.

"Who was that?" I ask. I'm in Reception, making Sammy laugh by hanging upside down on one of the brand new couches that got delivered yesterday to replace the gross ones.

Mom shakes her head. "That," she says, "was a woman who wanted to know if we have any wheelchair-accessible rooms. She's bringing her husband or someone to be healed."

"Healed? Wouldn't they stay at the hospital?"

"They're not coming to be healed at the hospital."

"Then where?"

"At the drive-in."

I sit up, the blood whooshing in my head. The drive-in?

"I need a Tylenol," Mom says, rubbing her palm and then her temples. "This place is giving me a headache."

I remember reading in one of Kate's articles that some people believe the Virgin Mary appears to help heal sick people.

I didn't even imagine that people would come to the drive-in to be healed. I wonder what's wrong with the woman's husband that the doctors can't fix.

My stomach twinges and I'm not sure if it's because Uncle Mordy has scheduled another swim lesson at noon or because, well, because some woman is bringing her husband to be healed by a fake Virgin Mary apparition.

I hope they're not coming from too far away.

I head to the pool just before noon, wishing I had turned down Mr. Whitley's late-morning grilled cheese sandwich with extra cheese and tomato after I peeled three huge bowls of grapes. Maria's in Reception, wiping the hand prints off the glass door.

"Hola, Miri," she says. Her face is shiny from sweat and the pieces of hair that have fallen out of her ponytail are stuck to her skin. She points to my bathing suit. "Swim lesson today?"

I make a face. "What's bathing suit in Spanish?"

"Traje de baño."

I try the words out. The way Maria pronounces the middle of *traje* sounds like the letter *chet* in Hebrew. I bet Maria could say challah the right way.

"What about drown?" I say.

"Por favor!" she says. "You are being *ridícula.*" Which clearly means ridiculous, which I am clearly not being because my legs are already starting to feel heavy and heavy legs don't lead to swimming, they lead to drowning.

Uncle Mordy comes out of the pool room.

"Es hora de aprender a nadar!" he says. He has a terrible accent but it's definitely Spanish.

"Dios mio!" says Maria. "You speak Spanish?" She laughs. "Another miracle!"

"Yep," says Uncle Mordy. "But it is 12:10 and my niece is still dry and I will not be distracted." He points his finger at me. *"A la piscina, rápido!"*

He pretends to whip me with the towel he is holding and I scoot past him into the pool room. I turn as he follows me in and see Maria staring at him. She looks impressed.

"To your thighs this time," Uncle Mordy says as I take my time folding my towel and lining up my flip-flops under one of the plastic chairs lining the sides of the room.

I take one step at a time into the water, getting up to my knees without a problem. Maybe I *can* do this.

But before I can go down one more step, my legs turn to trees and grow roots into the tiles.

"Come on, just one more."

The roots turn into cement blocks and there's no way I can even lift my foot up, let alone step down to the next step.

Uncle Mordy stands at the bottom of the steps, holding his arms out. "You can do it, Miriam."

I stay where I am.

"You learned all that Spanish in high school?" I ask him.

"Well, a few years of it in high school and then in college, and then I spent a summer in Spain doing research on *conversos* for grad school."

"What's *conversos*?"

"*Conversos* were Jews who were forced to convert to Catholicism in Spain, over five hundred years ago. But some of them still practiced Judaism secretly."

"Jews were forced to convert to Catholicism?"

Maybe that's why Mom acts so weird around Maria and Father Donovan. And why she freaked out when I was wearing Maria's necklace. But five hundred years is a long time ago, way before she was born. You'd think she'd be over it by now.

"Don't think I don't know what you're doing," Uncle Mordy says.

"What?"

"Distracting me from the matter at hand. Come on, one more step."

"Maria is really smart, don't you think?" I get my toes to wiggle, but that's about all.

"She certainly is."

"And pretty," I add, ignoring Uncle Mordy's out-stretched hands.

"Yes, that too."

"You know," I say, forcing one foot up off the bottom and then putting it back down, "she's going to be a doctor."

"Really? I didn't know that. That's awesome." He tugs gently on my hands. "One more step. You've got this."

Something is squeezing my chest and making it hard to breathe. I shake my head hard.

"Okay, let's just hang out on this step for a little bit longer. Deep breaths, remember?"

I take a couple of really deep breaths and feel my heart slow down a little.

"You're doing great, Miriam. Just one more step."

Uncle Mordy says it like he's telling Sammy to take one more bite of broccoli.

Fine.

I close my eyes and step down to the next step, and before I can even feel the water on my thighs, I'm out of the pool, grabbing a towel and drying off.

Uncle Mordy laughs and shakes his head. "I guess that counts."

He does a shallow dive from the steps into the water and waves his hand at me even though his face is in the water.

Swim lesson over. I may not have learned to swim today, but I did learn that Uncle Mordy speaks Spanish for real and that Maria looked very impressed.

If Maria and Uncle Mordy started dating, then she won't leave the Jewel, even if people stop coming to see the Virgin Mary at the drive-in.

That would be another miracle.

11

It's Friday night. All the guests we are expecting at the motel today have already arrived and gotten their keys. I set the table for dinner earlier with the fancy dishes that Mom finally unpacked. I let Sammy help by putting a napkin on everyone's chair.

Uncle Mordy's been ordering kosher chicken from a store in Spartanburg and today we made challah together, which we had to start in the morning because it had to rise twice — once before we braided it into loaves and then again after. We made an extra one to give to Mr. Whitley.

Wait until he tastes how much better it is compared to the bakery ones. I'm going to convince him to make his French toast with challah next.

Mom closes the dining-room door. The dining room is only open to guests for breakfast, but Mom still hangs a Do Not Disturb sign on it so no one will wander in. Because sundown is so late in the summer, Sammy's already gone to bed, which I'm kind of glad about. Mom puts the baby monitor in the middle of the table, so we'll hear him if he wakes up.

It will be nice to have Mom and Dad to myself for a little bit. At home, we used to play board games or watch a movie together in the evening after Sammy fell asleep. I miss that.

We light the candles and we're just about to say kiddush — the blessing over the wine and grape juice — when the bell downstairs tinkles.

"Yoo-hoo!" I hear through the closed door.

"It's Mrs. Whitley!" I say. "Can we invite her to dinner? Please?" I look back and forth from Mom to Dad. I would have asked to invite Kate but she's sleeping over at a friend's in Brookdale.

Mom shakes her head. "I don't think so, Miriam."

I look at Dad. "Please?"

Dad looks at Mom. "Why not, Deborah? It would be good to get to know our neighbors better."

"No," Mom says, rubbing her scar. "Shabbat dinner is family time."

"But at home —"

"Yoo-hoo!" Mrs. Whitley calls again. "Anyone home?"

I open the dining-room door as Mrs. Whitley reaches the top of the stairs. She's wearing a light blue dress that I haven't seen before and she's washed the flour out of her hair. Mr. Whitley's behind her. I almost don't recognize him in a button-down shirt, without his apron.

"Sorry to bother on your Sabbath," she says. "We're on our way to church for a meeting but I wanted to drop this by first."

She holds out a bottle of wine. "One of our friends had a wine store a few years ago. He brought us some bottles when he closed it, but neither of us are big wine drinkers. This one is from Israel."

Dad takes the bottle from behind me. "That's very thoughtful, thank you. We'll enjoy it tonight, in fact."

Mom joins us at the door, looking relieved. "Thank you, Myrna. That's kind of you."

"*Shabbat shalom,*" I say. "That's what we say on Shabbat. *Shalom* means peace. And hello and goodbye."

"Very versatile," Mr. Whitley says. *"Shabbat shalom."*

"Shabbat shalom," says Mrs. Whitley, as they head back down the stairs.

Uncle Mordy waits until he hears the bell and then says, "I heard about this meeting. Did you know that there's a bishop coming to help determine if the Virgin Mary apparition is to be considered real or not?"

I let out a gasp.

"You okay, Miriam?" asks Dad as he uncorks the bottle of wine.

"Just hungry," I say quickly. "Can we make kiddush now?"

"What *mishegas*," says Mom, using the Yiddish word for nonsense.

"This *mishegas* is filling our motel," says Dad. "Don't forget that."

Mom shakes her head, but she's smiling. Dad puts his arm around her and squeezes and she giggles. They look relaxed for the first time since we got here.

I stare at the challah cover in the middle of the table, covering the two challahs, waiting their turn.

"What happens if the bishop thinks the apparition isn't real?" I ask.

Dad shrugs. "I don't know. But either way, I think we'll be okay. I was reading about apparitions in other places, and even if the Church thinks they aren't real, people still come to see them."

I'm trying to figure out how they can tell if it's real or not. And what happens if they figure out that someone faked it?

I need to talk to Kate, who is in Brookdale at her friend's until sometime tomorrow afternoon.

We all stand up to say kiddush, finally. Uncle Mordy holds up the cup, filled almost to overflowing with the wine that the Whitleys brought, and says the blessing. We all take a sip and then Mom takes the challahs in her hands and says *hamotzi*, the blessing over bread.

As she cuts the challah and passes it around, I watch the Shabbat candles flicker on the counter.

At home, this is my favorite time of the week. But here, the candles feel like two eyes watching me, like they can tell what I did.

Kate told me about confession. She says some Catholics go every week, but her family goes only once a year, around Easter. You go into a special booth, like a closet, which is connected to another booth where Father Donovan sits, so they can hear each other but not see each other. It's supposed to be private and you don't have to say your name, but Kate says it's a small town and for sure he recognizes everyone's voice.

I explained to her about Yom Kippur, when Jews fast and pray in synagogue all day, thinking about the bad things they did the past year and what they need to do to be a better person. We're supposed to ask forgiveness from the person we hurt. We don't confess to the rabbi though.

I asked Kate if faking a Virgin Mary apparition is a sin you'd have to confess at confession.

"Yep," she said. "But luckily, Easter is nine months away."

The next morning, Mom wakes me all chirpy and tells me we're going to synagogue and I should put on something nice. I find a yellow sundress and get Sammy into a pair of navy shorts and a striped shirt.

I have a quick breakfast and then we head off in the car to Spartanburg. Uncle Mordy can't come because he doesn't drive on Shabbat. He spends the day relaxing. No screens, no phone, no using money. Uncle Mordy says Shabbat is how he recharges his batteries. And everyone's batteries are running pretty low since we got so busy.

Maria slept at a friend's last night but came back to watch Reception while we're gone, since Uncle Mordy can't answer the phone on Shabbat. All the rooms are full, so we're not expecting anyone new, but the phone keeps ringing with people calling to see if there's a vacancy. We're booked for the next three weeks, with a whole bunch of people on a wait list.

I'm not too excited about synagogue, but it's probably the only way I'm getting out of Greenvale anytime soon. No one has time to do anything but work. Except for a trip to the supermarket in town and biking with Kate, I haven't even left the motel, unless you count going next door to the diner and down the street to the gas station.

I really want to go over to the diner first to find out what happened at the meeting last night, but Mom tells me to get into the car. On the highway we pass a bunch of signs advertising other motels as we get closer to Spartanburg.

The synagogue is a big brick building with a parking lot, really different from back home where everyone walks or takes the subway to services. I sit and listen while someone reads from the big Torah scroll and the cantor sings some prayers.

Then the rabbi starts her sermon.

She tells a story from the Torah about a man named Balaam who was a sorcerer. Balaam isn't Jewish, and his king tells him to go and curse the Jews. Balaam agrees, but then God tells him not to. The king convinces him to go curse them anyway, but on the way, Balaam's donkey sees an angel in the road and stops, refusing to walk past it. Balaam can't see the angel and beats the donkey for stopping. He keeps at it until the donkey asks Balaam why he is beating him. After that, Balaam can see the angel. And when he gets to where he is supposed to curse the Jews, a blessing comes out of his mouth instead.

It all sounds totally unbelievable. If Judaism believes in angels and talking donkeys, then what's so weird about people believing that the Virgin Mary appeared on a movie screen?

The rabbi never says why Balaam wants to curse the Jews. What did they ever do to him? Maybe this is what Mom was talking about when she said people do hateful things to Jews.

The rabbi is still talking and I try hard to pay attention again.

"Of all the things we are blessed with, I believe the most important blessing of all is the blessing of choice. *We* are the ones who choose the path we take with our lives. *We* are the ones who choose the kind of person we will become. This is an enormous responsibility, yes, but the fact that we get to choose is truly a blessing, one that we should never take for granted.

"Life is not simply what happens to us. Life is what we *do* with what happens to us." She pauses a moment, looking around the room.

"Choose wisely," she finishes. *"Shabbat shalom."*

Everyone opens their siddur, the prayer book, to continue with the service.

I open mine but can't concentrate on the prayers. I couldn't do anything about moving to a dump of a motel even though I didn't want to. I didn't have a choice, but now I'm doing something to make it better.

I ignore the fact that my choice involves lying and fooling people. I'm guessing that's not what the rabbi meant.

After services, the rabbi comes over and introduces herself as Rabbi Yael. She asks if we're visiting someone in the community.

131

"No, we live on the outskirts of Greenvale," Dad says. "We bought and moved into the Jewel Motor Inn at the end of June."

The rabbi hasn't heard of the Jewel. But she has heard about the apparition.

"Father Donovan's been working overtime, that's for sure," she says.

"You know Father Donovan?" I ask.

"Sure," she says. "All the clergy in the area get together a couple of times a year to talk about various concerns in the community. There aren't that many of us, and we try to collaborate on an inter-denominational — that means involving different religions — project each year or two."

As we head to the next room to have cookies and fruit, I wonder if me and Kate and the drive-in would be considered inter-denominational collaboration.

I'm pushing Sammy on the swings after we get back from synagogue and have lunch when a car drives into the parking lot and pulls into the spot right in front of Reception — the one with the blue-and-white wheelchair sign painted on it. A woman gets out and pulls a wheelchair out of the back and brings it around to the side of the car and helps someone get into it.

When the wheelchair turns around, I see that it's not her husband in it. It's a kid.

I'm not sure how old he is because he's sitting down, but his face looks like he might be around my age, maybe a little older. The top of his body looks healthy, but his legs are kind of small and thin and his shorts look too big on him.

"Mi-wam! Push me!"

I turn to give him another push as the woman pushes the wheelchair into Reception. By the time they come out, Sammy's tired of the swings and wants to play in the sandbox. I feel the boy watching me as I lift Sammy out of the swing and plop him down on the sand. When I turn around, he waves. I give a small wave back. He smiles and goes into Room 101, the room right next to Reception.

I see Maria wheeling her cart down the balcony on the second floor. She waves and calls down to me to come up and keep her company.

I wonder how you say wheelchair in Spanish.

The kid with the wheelchair is at breakfast the next morning. He must have used the service elevator to get up here, the one that the delivery people use. He wheels around with his plate on his lap. When he's filled it with hard-boiled eggs and whole wheat toast, he wheels up to the only free table, in the corner, and puts the plate on it.

He sees me and waves again and I wave back from behind the counter where Mom and I are laying out more bagels. There are so many guests now that the bakery man comes every day instead of every other day. I'm putting the bagels in a pattern on the tray: first a poppy seed one, then a sesame seed, then plain, then cinnamon raisin. It helps me not die of boredom.

"Can I go eat breakfast with him?" I ask Mom. I had breakfast early when Sammy woke up, but serving the guests always makes me hungry again.

"Let the guests eat in peace," says Mom.

"No, that would be great," a voice says. It's the boy's mother. She takes a poppy seed bagel and messes up my pattern.

"It would be nice for Anton to have some company his own age. And I have to go back to the room to make a phone call in five minutes."

Mom nods, so I grab a bagel, a cream cheese packet and a banana that looks like it might be ripe enough to eat and go over to his table. He's straightened out his wheelchair so he's facing forward, but the table leg is in the way and he needs to stretch his arm way out to reach his food. It doesn't look too comfortable.

I wonder what's wrong with his legs, but I'm not sure if it's okay to ask.

"I'm Miriam," I say. "Anton, right?"

"Sounds like you've met my mom already. Do you actually work here?"

"I live here. With my family. In Room 109."

"That's totally cool," he says. "I've never heard of a kid living in a motel before. Do you get to raid the vending machines and order room service whenever you want? And people must leave stuff behind all the time. I once forgot a pair of brand-new sneakers at a motel."

Hmm. Maybe it is cool to live here, even if it's not the Plaza. And the Jewel is beginning to shape up a bit. Uncle Mordy gave the halls a new coat of paint and Maria washed all the windows so you can actually tell it's daytime when you're inside. We've all been working really hard and it's finally starting to show.

"No room service here," I say. "Which is good, because I'd probably get roped into delivering coffee to people at six in the morning."

He grins at me, reaching for a butter packet that's a little too far away on the table. I lean over and push it closer to him so he can grab it.

"Thanks. Most people would just hand it to me. I like that you didn't do that."

I shrug. I hadn't thought about it, really.

His mom comes over, her bagel wrapped in a napkin.

"Have everything you need, hon? I need to go back to the room to make a call."

"All set," Anton tells her. He ducks as she tries to kiss him on the head. "Mom!"

"Where do *you* live?" I ask when she walks off.

"Chicago. It took like ten hours to get here, including stops."

"You drove ten hours to see the apparition? That's —" I bite my tongue. "I mean …"

I'm not sure what I mean. That I can't believe he'd drive ten hours to see a Virgin Mary apparition? Or to see a fake Virgin Mary apparition?

"I know. But my mom says there's this place in, like, Europe or somewhere, where these kids saw

136

the Virgin Mary appear. She says that some people who go there get cured of whatever's wrong with them. She wanted to take me there when I was a baby, but we couldn't afford it."

"Oh." I can't think of anything else to say.

"She's always looking for a miracle. She's dragged me to, like, three or four of these since I was a kid."

"And?"

"Still got the wheelchair, right?"

I cringe at his words and take a bite of my banana. It's not ripe enough after all, and gives me an icky feeling on my teeth. I don't want to spit it out in front of Anton, so I swallow it and try not to make a face.

"Don't look so freaked out. What my mom doesn't understand is that my life is fine the way it is. I don't need to walk. What I really need is a Zabulon Sport."

"A what?"

"A Zabulon Sport. With turbo castors and Top-Grip handrims and Vitalux SLX wheels. In red."

"Is that some kind of motorcycle?"

Anton laughs. "Nah, it's a basketball wheelchair."

Wow. "You play basketball in a wheelchair?"

"Sure. You need a special one though. And the good ones cost like three thousand."

I look at the wheelchair he's sitting in. "Three thousand dollars?"

"Not this one. This is a crappy cheap one my mom got for traveling. I have a really good one at home. But it's just for getting around. Insurance doesn't pay for basketball wheelchairs."

"That stinks." I think about how when I want to play kickball at school or go biking with Kate, I can just go do it.

"Yeah. Maybe when we get back later I can show you some pictures. We're here until Friday. Room 101."

I already know what room he's in and how long he's staying, of course, but I don't tell him that. His mom comes back and says they need to go.

"See you later, then?" he asks.

"Yeah. See you later."

Now I have even more questions. Has a Virgin Mary apparition ever really healed someone? There are miracles in Judaism, but they all happened a long time ago. Like when the Jews left Egypt and the Red Sea split to let Moses and all the Jews through, but not the Egyptians who were chasing them. And Chanukah celebrates how after the Jews were attacked by the Greeks and won, they only had enough oil to light the menorah in the ancient Temple for one day, but it lasted for eight, until the Jews had time to make more.

Miracles like that don't happen anymore. Unless you count me getting up to my thighs in the pool. Which probably wouldn't be called a miracle.

But it should be.

12

I wake up late the next day after a dream about the Virgin Mary and people waking from the dead and walking around like zombies. I realize I need to do some research.

There's an old computer on a rickety table in the corner of the dining room. It's supposed to be for guests, but since everyone comes with their own laptop or phone, it just sits there.

Uncle Mordy's in the dining room, cleaning up after breakfast.

"Can I use the computer?"

"Sure, but can you help me first? I have to get into town to the hardware store this morning."

I take over setting the tables for tomorrow morning while Uncle Mordy fills the cereal containers and cleans the waffle maker from all the drips that went down the sides because people don't follow directions and pour in too much batter.

While I work I review the Spanish words I know in my head. I put each piece of silverware in its place: *tenedor, cuchillo, cuchara.* Napkin is *servilleta.* I wipe the *sal* and *pimienta* shakers down just like I do at the diner.

"Thanks a million, Miriam," Uncle Mordy says as he leaves. He doesn't mention another swimming lesson. Sweet.

I ignore the sign that says No Food or Drink While on Computer and fill a glass with orange juice.

The computer takes forever to boot up, but when it does I do a search for "Jesus."

The first link that pops up says that Jesus was a Jewish rabbi from the Galilee in Israel. I had no idea that Jesus was even Jewish, let alone a rabbi. Does that mean that Catholics and Jews come from the same roots? I wonder if Mom knows that.

I type in "Virgin Mary apparitions" and start clicking.

I don't understand everything, but it's clear that there have been a lot of Virgin Mary apparitions all over the world. Most of the apparitions are visions, or ghost-like appearances that only a few people see. But there are a few others where people saw the Virgin Mary appear on something like a piece of wood or a canvas.

Some of these were hundreds of years ago, but I read about some that were just a couple of years ago. A few have even been in places I've heard of, like one in a bush in Philadelphia and another on a farm in Maryland.

I click another link and there's a photo of a piece of toast.

I push back in my chair and tilt my head back and forth. It does kind of look like there's a face on the toast. The parts of the bread that are more brown form the hair and the eyes, which are kind of looking down toward the crust on the bottom. I can even make out a nose and a mouth.

"Ah, classic case of face pareidolia," says a voice behind me, making me jump and knock over my juice.

"Oh, shoot, sorry!" says the voice. I grab napkins

from the tables and frantically mop up the OJ heading toward the keyboard.

The woman behind me has a key card in her mouth as she uses both hands to help. She's young like Maria.

"I'm Susan," she says as we go over to the sink to wash our sticky hands. "Sorry to startle you. I was looking for my room and I got nosy."

"I'm Miriam. Which room?"

"Huh?"

"Which room are you looking for?"

"Oh — 114."

"Go to the right, halfway down the corridor. Next to the ice machine."

"Great, thanks," she says. She picks up her suitcase.

"Wait," I say. "What is par … pari …?"

"Pareidolia." She pronounces it *par-ay-doh-lia*.

"Yeah, that."

"It's a psychological phenomenon in which we perceive a vague or random stimulus as being significant."

I stare at her.

"It means that we tend to see patterns — especially faces — in things that are random. Like when you look at a full moon and see a face. You know, the Man in the Moon."

"Oh." I've seen that.

She points at the computer screen. "Like that photograph, for example. That's a famous one."

"Really?"

"Really. What does it look like to you?"

"Like a woman's face."

"Right, the Virgin Mary. That got a lot of attention when it was first publicized. But look." She puts her finger on the screen so that it covers the woman's eyes. All of a sudden the rest of her face just looks like a bunch of random brown spots. Like any other piece of toast.

"Or take this." She grabs a salt shaker from one of the tables and holds it so I can see the little holes on top. "Can you see a face here?"

I don't at first, but then suddenly I see how the holes make a smiling face with wavy hair on top.

"Our brains are wired to see faces in things. We make them up. That's the topic for my grad thesis. I came here to interview some of the people coming to the drive-in."

My brain is going a million miles an hour trying

to keep up. She's here to study people who are coming to see the apparition that Kate and I made up.

"So you don't think it's real," I say carefully.

Susan wrinkles her nose. "Well, it's real to the people who see it, but it's not the Virgin Mary. It's just their minds playing tricks on them."

Or me and Kate playing tricks on them.

She picks up her suitcase. "To the right, you said?"

"Uh-huh." I look back at the photo of the toast. Without Susan's finger there, it looks like a face again.

A thought creeps up.

Kate and I saw the face of a woman with long hair on our own. Which must be face pareidolia. Then Kate added the cross so people would think the face was the Virgin Mary.

So we didn't really fake a Virgin Mary apparition. Not totally. The face was already there.

I need to talk to Kate.

Maybe she doesn't need to go to confession after all.

My stomach grumbles. All this staring at toast has made me hungry.

I'm in the mood for real food, not candy or chips from the vending machine. I open the small fridge in the back — the one we keep our own food in — but all that's in it is a wilted lettuce and some fish sticks cut into Sammy-sized pieces. Someone needs to start a grocery delivery service in Greenvale.

I head over to the diner. Mrs. Whitley is outside directing a big white truck as it backs up to the delivery door. The driver hops out and unloads two big crates. Mrs. Whitley pries one open and inside are bunches and bunches of big, round, deep-purple grapes. There must be thousands! I breathe in deeply, holding the sweetness in my lungs, and imagine purple spreading though my body.

"Nothing like the smell of Concord grapes," Mrs. Whitley says, closing her eyes and breathing in just like me. "Wait until next month, when the local grapes are ready. You'll be dreaming in purple."

Mrs. Whitley tripled her order because of all the people coming to Greenvale. Her pies made the paper again. This time the article said they were the best pies in all of upstate New York, not just the county. Now people stop at the diner for a slice on their way to the drive-in, and then pick up a whole pie to take home on their way back.

The pile of five-dollar bills in my dresser is growing. I haven't spent any of them since I never go anywhere. And I can get all the Ring Pops I want for free with the vending machine key.

My stomach growls again.

Mrs. Whitley laughs. "Help me get these grapes into the kitchen and then we'll get you some lunch."

"Thanks," I tell her.

Inside I can hear Mr. Whitley singing in the kitchen. Father Donovan is sitting in one of the booths, reading the paper with a cup of coffee and a slice of pie.

"Hi, Miriam!" he says.

"The usual?" Mrs. Whitley asks me.

I nod.

"Back in a jiffy," she says, heading into the kitchen.

Father Donovan moves his newspaper over so I can sit down across from him.

"This pie is heaven-sent," he says. His napkin is stained deep purple.

"Can I ask you a question?"

"Sure. Shoot."

I think carefully first. "Do people really believe that the face at the drive-in is the Virgin Mary?"

"Well, given how many people have come to Greenvale in the past few of weeks, I'd say a lot of them do. Or they want to believe."

I bite my lip. "But couldn't it just be a face? Why is it so important to people that it's the Virgin Mary?" I study his expression.

"Good question," he says, just like the rabbi at Bubbie's synagogue does. "Some people believe the Virgin Mary comes back to give us messages. Or to help us through hard times."

"Susan — she's in Room 114 — says that people's minds are playing tricks on them. That it's something called pareidolia."

Father Donovan nods. "I know."

"You know?"

"Yes. She called me last week and asked to interview me for her thesis."

I think about that for a minute.

"So, what do you think?" I ask, not sure if I want the answer.

He takes a swallow of his coffee. "I'll admit I have my doubts, but I don't know for sure. God works in mysterious ways. But what I am certain of is that what matters isn't whether the apparition is real or not, but what it means to the people who see it."

Mrs. Whitley appears with a glass of lemonade and a grilled cheese sandwich. She's wearing the new apron that Mr. Whitley gave her, which says Have A Grape Day! over an outline of a bunch of grapes.

The sandwich is made with challah, of course. The cheese has oozed out of a couple of holes in the bread and gotten darker in those spots, almost like two eyes.

Mr. Whitley liked using challah for his grilled cheese so much that he put it on the menu. He calls it the Miriam Special and now he orders challah every week from the kosher bakery in Spartanburg. Now I can hear him whistling in the kitchen.

Whenever I feel bad about the drive-in, I think about how happy Mr. and Mrs. Whitley are.

Father Donovan's phone dings and he pulls it out of his pocket.

"Sorry to cut our conversation short, but I've got an appointment with the local bishop and Officer Mike. I look forward to more of your questions another time."

He stands up and hands Mrs. Whitley a few bills.

"Delicious pie, as always."

My stomach unclenches a little. If it doesn't matter to Father Donovan if the apparition is real or not, then maybe it doesn't matter to all the people coming here.

Maybe it's not so terrible what we did.

Three o'clock finally comes and Kate finds me on the Reception couch reading a book a guest left behind called *A Guide to the Trees and Wildflowers of Upstate New York*, trying not to die of boredom. She's sweaty and dirty from playing softball at camp and the bike ride over.

"I think I'm melting," she says.

It's check-in time so Reception is starting to get crowded.

"Do you care that we never go swimming?" I ask her as we walk over to Room 109, the only place we can get some privacy, at least when Sammy's not napping.

Kate knows I'm scared of water and about the swimming lessons with Uncle Mordy. Even though she can't imagine being afraid of water, she never laughs or makes fun of me like some of the kids at Lekha's birthday party did.

"Nah, it's fine. I go every day at camp anyway. And outdoor pools are more fun in the summer anyway." She goes to splash her face in the bathroom.

Sometimes I wish I could go to camp with her. The motel is busier now so it's a little more fun. Maria and I have a contest to see who will find the weirdest thing that people leave behind. I found a ukulele under a bed but then Maria found this guy's teeth in a cup on the nightstand and Mom had to mail them back to him in a padded envelope.

And there's Anton, at least for now.

But still, it would be nice to be around some more kids. I started to ask Dad about camp a few days ago, but he was too busy to talk, and that night I heard him and Mom talking about expenses and all the things at the Jewel that needed to be fixed or replaced and I felt bad about asking them to spend money on camp.

"Father Donovan was at the diner today," I tell her after she plops on Sammy's bed and pulls a pack of chewing gum out of her pocket.

"I think he's there every day," she laughs, tossing me a stick. "Grandma's best customer." She admires the new posters I put on the walls along with the now-framed photos of me and Dahlia and Lekha

151

and inspects the holders I made for my markers and pencils out of soda cans that guests threw out.

I tell her about Susan and pareidolia. And a little about Anton.

"Wow. How old is he? What's wrong with his legs? Does his mother really think there will be a miracle?" she asks.

"I don't know," I say to all three questions. I don't really want to talk about him with her. "I only spoke to him once."

"But he's the most exciting thing that's happened here since the motel reopened."

"Exciting? Because he uses a wheelchair?"

"You know what I mean."

"No, I don't. What do you mean?"

She chews her gum and doesn't say anything.

"The wheelchair isn't a big deal," I tell her. "He's just a regular kid. He even plays basketball."

"Okay, okay," Kate says. "Sorry. Why are you so grumpy anyway?"

"I'm not grumpy. I'm just worried." I tell her what Father Donovan said about not knowing if the apparition is real or not and maybe it not mattering anyway. "Do you think it would matter to him if he knew what we did?"

"Father Donovan's pretty cool, for a priest," she says. "I wouldn't worry about it." She blows a big bubble that breaks all over her face and I burst out laughing.

She clearly isn't worrying about it, so I decide not to either.

I watch Sammy for a while after breakfast the next day. I feel bad that I haven't spent much time with him lately so I tell him we're going to do something special and he jumps up and down.

I take him over to the diner. He picks a booth and I order two lemonades. Mrs. Whitley puts Sammy's in a plastic cup but of course he wants to drink from mine. He makes a pile with the sugar packets and I pretend the salt shaker is a monster and knock them over. He squeals with laughter and piles them up again and again.

He flips onto his stomach to slide off his seat and comes around to my side. I lift him up next to me and hug and kiss him until he says, "I tired." He leans his head against my side.

I take him back to our room and we snuggle until the babysitter arrives and then, for once, I have nothing to do. Kate's at camp as usual and Anton's car isn't in the parking lot. Mrs. Whitley's made enough pies for a couple of days.

I find Maria in one of the upstairs rooms and offer to help her. With so many people coming and going, it's hard to get all the rooms ready by check-in time every day.

She vacuums the floor and cleans the bathroom while I replace the little shampoo bottles and put out new soaps. Maria takes the partly used ones and when she has a full box she takes them to the food bank in Spartanburg for people who need them. I empty the garbage cans and put clean towels on the racks.

While we work, she teaches me new words: *el champú*, *el jabón*, *la toalla*. I've lost count of how many words I've learned since I got here. I still can't put them into real sentences though, except for *"Tarta de uvas para postre, por favor,"* which means "Grape pie for dessert, please."

If a guest is staying another night, we just straighten up and clean the bathroom. Some guests leave their rooms a total mess, stuff hanging out of their suitcases and wet towels all over the floor. In one room we found a half-eaten pizza in the bathtub. These guests probably don't even notice that there are new, dry towels folded in the bathroom when they get back.

Other guests are super neat, hanging their clothes in the little closet by color and lining up their toothbrushes and toothpaste in size order next to the sink. I try to put things back exactly where they left them after I wipe down the sink and counter, since they will definitely notice.

A few people leave money on the dresser when they leave, as a tip. Maria tries to share it with me when I help her, but I've got my five-dollar bills from working at the diner, and I know Maria needs the money for school.

We're cleaning Room 102 when I hear voices in the next room, the one where Anton and his mother are staying. I didn't even hear their car pull up.

I'm not allowed to knock on the guests' doors because Mom's big on privacy, so I open the door of the room we're in and prop it open with the garbage can. This way I can see if Anton comes out. The air outside the motel is so hot that I'm glad I'm inside cleaning, where at least there's air conditioning.

I can hear the shower running in Anton's room, and then I hear the door to the room open. I put my armful of dirty towels in the laundry bag hanging from Maria's cart and go outside.

I jump back just in time to save myself as Anton flies by in his wheelchair. He's barreling down the strip of pavement that separates the rooms on the ground floor from the parking lot, his arms pushing hard and fast on the rims of his wheels. When he reaches the end, he spins around and does this pop-wheelie thing and heads back toward me. He stops short just a few inches from my toes, a big grin on his face.

"Don't tell my mom. She doesn't like it when I spin this thing. But I don't want my arms to get all weak while I'm out here."

I don't think there's much chance of that. Anton's arms look super strong, all muscly, not like my puny ones.

"Where were you?" I ask.

"The drive-in," he says.

I try to read his expression but it's pretty flat.

I want to ask what he thinks about the Virgin Mary, almost forgetting that there is no Virgin Mary. I stare at the ground, and then worry that he thinks I'm staring at his legs so I look up, out at the playground. The babysitter is pushing Sammy on the swing and he waves at me. There's a couple watching another little kid in the new sandbox that Uncle Mordy built.

"Just looked like a peeling movie screen to me," he says, like he's reading my mind. "But my mom thought it was amazing. She got down on her knees and prayed like her life depended on it. She wants to go back every day until we leave. Guess she thinks I need a quadruple dose of miracle or something."

He doesn't look sad when he says this, just tired or something. He wheels up to his door and pokes his head in.

"She's still in the shower. Wanna race?"

"Race?"

"Yeah. You with your legs, me with the chair."

It doesn't really seem fair, but Anton is already heading to the Reception door, so I follow him.

He points to the other end of the strip, where Mom planted some new daisies in a big pot to replace the dead ones that were here when we arrived. "First one to the flowerpot wins."

He's dreaming. How could he possibly beat me?

He backs up a couple of feet. "Let me get some momentum going. You start running when I reach you, okay?"

That seems fair. He starts moving toward me, yelling, "Go!" just as he reaches me. I pull ahead right away, but by Room 105 I can feel him right at my heels.

How can he possibly go that fast?

He's ahead by Room 108 but I give it all I've got and start to pass him. Just as we reach the flower-pot he swerves toward me and does this zigzag thing and cuts me off. I lose my balance and fall down hard on my hands and knees.

What a jerk!

I inspect my bleeding knee and pick the gravel out of it, trying to hold back tears. Anton wheels over.

"Shoot," he says. "You okay?" He flips his brake handles and puts his hand out.

"Cheater," I say, ignoring his hand. He *is* a regular kid.

"Sorry," he says. "Let's call it a tie."

"A tie?" I say. "You cut me off on purpose." I look up at him. I wonder if this is how I look to him when I'm standing.

He leans forward so his hand is closer. "I *am* sorry. I can be a jerk sometimes. Just, people don't usually call me on it. You definitely won."

I glare at him a few more seconds and then reach out and grab his hand. He leans back and pulls me up. I feel the sting in my knee.

His mother comes to the door and tells him to get ready to go to lunch. I head off to find a Band-Aid. By the time I find one, I'm more amazed than mad.

Yeah, Anton cheated at the end, but honestly? It was a really close race.

13

The next morning there's a note under my door. I'm hoping it's from Anton, but when I open it I see a drawing of a pool with a stick figure standing on the steps with the water up to her waist.

Swim lesson 10:00. Be there or be square! it says, with a smiley face under it.

For real? *Be there or be square?* My uncle must be older than I thought.

There's no sign of Anton or his mother at breakfast. I check with Dad at Reception, and they are still booked to be here until the weekend.

The clock behind the reception counter says 9:00. One hour until I have to get back in the pool.

An hour later, which feels like two minutes, I'm watching Susan in the pool doing laps, while Uncle Mordy waits in the water for me. At the deep end of each lap she does a cool somersault-flip move so that she's facing the right way to start the next lap. At the shallow end she just turns around.

She waves at me, barely lifting her face out of the water. With her yellow and turquoise bathing suit she reminds me of the fish swimming back and forth in the aquarium at my dentist. My old dentist. I don't have a dentist here yet, probably because Mom and Dad are too busy to notice all the Ring Pops and sugar cereal I've been eating.

I step into the water, two steps right away, the water at my knees.

Easy peasy.

Susan lifts herself out of the side of the pool in one smooth motion, grabs her towel and leaves, winking at me as she goes out. I'm glad she won't be here to watch me.

Uncle Mordy takes my hand and leads me down one more step. I wait for my heart to start racing, but it doesn't.

Hmm. Maybe I *can* do this. Uncle Mordy tugs on my hand but I need another minute.

Maria pokes her head in, sees us in the pool, and waves. "Never mind, I'll find you later. *Chao!*"

Uncle Mordy waves back. *"Hasta luego."*

"It would be nice to have an aunt," I say, swirling the water around with my hands. "Especially one that spoke Spanish."

Uncle Mordy sits down on the step above me. I turn to face him and fight the urge to walk back up the steps and out of the water.

"You know that Maria isn't Jewish, right?" he says.

I nod. Of course I know that.

"And even though she's smart, and nice, and works hard —"

"And is pretty."

"And is pretty," Uncle Mordy continues, "and I enjoy being around her, I wouldn't marry anyone who wasn't Jewish."

"Why does that matter? Maria's a really good person."

He thinks for a minute.

"Well, I live a committed Jewish life, and it's important to me that the person I marry can share that with me. And when I have kids, I want to raise them with a commitment to a Jewish way of life.

Maria is committed to Catholicism, to a Catholic way of life."

"So? Couldn't you still get along being different religions?" I stay on my nice, comfortable step.

"It's not that we can't get along. We just believe in different things. And while I can be friends with someone who believes in different things than I do, it's a lot harder to be married to, and raise a family with, someone who is different in these big ways. Not everyone feels that way, and that's okay. But I do."

I pull away from him. That doesn't seem fair. Why does it have to matter to him what religion Maria is?

"I'm sorry to disappoint you," says Uncle Mordy. He has a big smile on his face.

I scowl at him. "Then why are you smiling?"

"Because you're in the water up to your waist."

I look down. He's right! The water is right at my belly button, which is weird because I don't even remember going down the last step. My fingertips are under the water, making it look like I have frog fingers. I scoot out of the water before my brain can realize where my body is.

I think while I dry myself off. Maria and Uncle Mordy are not going to get married. Anton is not going to get the miracle his mother wants.

But I am now officially halfway into the pool.

Mom's in Reception when we come out of the pool room and I tell her my news.

She claps her hands and gives me a big hug even though I'm still in my wet bathing suit. "That's amazing! You should do something fun to celebrate."

Which is perfect, because after I eat lunch, Anton finds me to say that he and his mother are going to Crystal Caverns at three o'clock. He invites me to come along. When I tell him that Kate is coming over he invites her too. When she gets here, Kate says she's been to the caverns a hundred times but she'll come anyway and I know it's because she wants to hang out with Anton.

I watch, curious, as Anton gets into the car.

With the car door full open, he rolls his chair right up to the passenger seat and locks his brakes. He flips up the armrest and puts a board from one end on the car's seat to the edge of the wheelchair seat, like a bridge. Then he grabs onto something inside the car that I can't see and pulls himself across the board and into the car. Once he's inside, he uses his hands to lift his legs into the car one at a time. He leans out and pops his chair's brake handles, pushes the wheelchair out of the way, and closes the door.

It's like a dance.

Kate and I sit in the back. Anton's mother doesn't say much. Anton told me earlier that they've gone to the drive-in two more times.

What if there really was a miracle? I wonder what it would look like. Would it start with Anton moving his toes, and then his feet? Or would it happen all at once?

Anton's telling us about a book about spelunking — exploring caves — that he read for school last year, but I'm not really paying attention. I'm imagining him just standing up and walking across the room. What would he do first? Run and jump? Go grab a basketball? Dance?

The parking lot at Crystal Caverns is almost full, but we get to park right near the entrance because Anton's car has a special license plate. I start to tell him how lucky he is to always get a good parking spot, but then I realize how that sounds.

Once Anton's out of the car, we go into the gift shop where they sell the tour tickets. There are posters of the inside of the cave along the walls of the shop. Rock hangs like icicles from the ceilings and glistening pillars grow up from the floor.

Anton's mother buys the tickets while Anton, Kate and I look around. There are T-shirts and snow globes, and there's a crate of smooth stones of every color that you can buy by the bag.

But my favorite things are the geodes: big brown rocks that look ugly and boring from the outside but inside have beautiful purple, pink and white crystals.

Some of the aisles are too narrow for Anton's wheelchair, so I bring stuff over for him to see.

When they call our tour, we head over to the back of the store where the guide, who looks like a high-school kid, is waiting. He looks at Anton and shakes his head.

"No strollers or wheelchairs. There's, like, two hundred stairs to get to the bottom."

"What?" says Anton's mother, waving the Crystal Caverns pamphlet in her hand. "It says right here that the cave is wheelchair accessible."

The kid shrugs. "Elevator's broken. The only way down right now is the stairs."

"Well, when will it be fixed?" Anton's mother demands.

"I don't know. The boss says it's too expensive and —"

"Too *expensive*?" Anton's mother's voice is loud now and people turn to look at us. The kid squirms.

Anton blows out a slow breath. "It's okay, Mom."

"It's not okay," she says.

They lock eyes for a few seconds and then she looks at me and Kate, then at the guide, and back to Anton, like she's doing some kind of calculation in her head. Her eyes are flashing. It's like someone put a new set of batteries in her.

Anton turns to me and Kate. "You guys go see the cave. I'll hang out up here. I need to pick out a present for my dad and sister anyway."

I didn't even know he had a sister. Is his dad hoping for a miracle too?

I search Anton's face but either he's not disappointed or he's really good at hiding it. I do a calculation of my own and realize I want to see the cave with Anton more than I want to see the cave.

"Nah," I say. "Let's just go back to the Jewel. Mrs. Whitley can always use help making pies these days. I bet you could help if you wanted."

"I have a better idea," Anton says. "Let's go swimming."

My stomach does flips. "Kate doesn't have a bathing suit with her," I say, giving her a look.

"Can't you lend her one?" Anton asks.

"I don't have an extra," I say, but Kate's shaking her head no anyway.

"I promised I'd be home for dinner. Some cousin is visiting from somewhere."

"I'm not really in the mood for swimming," I say. "And anyway, I was in the pool this morning."

"Aw, come on." Anton says. "I haven't been in the pool even once since we got here. And yes," he says, seeing my expression, "I can swim."

I spend the drive back to the motel trying to figure out how *not* to go swimming, but in the end, I agree. There's no way I'm going to tell him I'm afraid, when I have two good legs.

Back in my room, I put on my bathing suit and pull my shorts and T-shirt back over it because it's not like I'm going in, and head over to the pool.

I'm not even sure Anton was serious about the swimming. Can he really? I guess I'm curious.

Anton's already in the water when I get there. I have no idea how he got in, but his wheelchair is parked by the side of the pool and he's swimming laps, just like Susan does. His arms are doing the breast stroke but his legs don't kick. They just trail behind him as he moves through the water.

When he sees me, he swims over to the edge of the pool and hangs on the side, catching his breath.

"How did you get in?" I ask. "Where's your mom?"

"She went back to the room. Trust me, though, she'll be back to check on me every five seconds. Hey, do you have one of those pool noodles? Or water wings or something?"

There's a storage box in the corner with life jackets and stuff for the little kids. No water wings, but I pull out a green noodle.

"Perfect. Come in and help me get it under my legs. It's easier to swim if my legs can float."

"Um … I'm not wearing a suit."

"Sure you are. I can see the straps poking out of your shirt."

I pull at my T-shirt. "Can we do it from the shallow end?"

Anton swims over to the steps and grabs the metal railing that goes right down the middle. He floats on his stomach. "Come in and get the noodle right under my knees."

I pull off my shorts and go down three steps into the pool, which brings the water up to my thighs. I take deep breaths like Uncle Mordy taught me and remind myself that I went in even deeper than this before.

I can't quite reach Anton, so I take another deep breath and go down one more step, to the one I made it to last time. The water is up to my waist but I do my best not to think about that. I push the noodle under the water to get it under Anton's knees but before I get it into position it shoots up out of the water and into the air and lands back in the pool.

Anton cracks up. "At home I have a float that straps around my legs for when I go swimming. But this should work if we get it in the right place."

The noodle is floating right in the middle of the pool, where the deep end starts. Too far for me to reach from the steps or the side. Anton is still holding on to the railing and doesn't look like he's about to go get it. Any second he's going to notice that I'm not either.

I go back to the storage box and come back with an armful of noodles of different colors and lengths.

"Well, we have four more tries," I say.

It takes all four. But on the last one — yellow — the noodle stays put. Anton makes it to the other end of the pool and back without it popping out.

He swims much faster with the noodle. I wonder if he'd beat Susan in a race. Assuming he didn't cheat.

"You coming in?" he asks.

I shrug. "I guess I'm not in a swimming mood."

I sit down on the edge of the pool and dangle my movable legs over the side. I feel like crying. Why do I always feel like this around him?

He swims over to me, puts his hands on the side of the pool and uses his arms to pull himself out of the water, then twists himself around so he's sitting next to me on the ledge. The yellow noodle floats out to meet the other four in the middle of the pool.

My feet make figure eights in the water. Anton's just hang there.

"It's okay if you're scared, you know. There's lots of things I've been scared of until I tried them. Even wheelchair basketball, in the beginning."

I start to tell him I'm not scared, but all of a sudden I don't want to lie to him anymore. I tell him about the swimming lessons, if you could call them that, and the panic that takes over my body when I try to go all the way in. My muscles relax just talking to him about it.

"You'll do it when you're ready," he says, just like Uncle Mordy.

The door opens. It's Anton's mother.

"I'll be back in fifteen minutes to help you out," she says. "There's a special mass at the drive-in at four and then we need to start packing up. We go home tomorrow."

The air in the room is heavy when she leaves, like she's left some of her sadness behind.

Anton watches her leave.

"Maybe one day," he says quietly, "she'll realize that I don't need a miracle."

He smiles at me. "Things are pretty okay the way they are."

14

The next morning, when I pull open my curtain, I see Anton in the front seat of his car while his mom puts a suitcase in the trunk. I throw on some clothes, grab a pad of paper from the desk in the room and go outside.

His mother slams the trunk closed and heads into Reception with her key card.

I stick my head through the open car window.

"You're leaving," I say.

"Yeah," he says. "I looked for you in the dining room. My mom decided to leave earlier than we planned."

"Here's the address of the motel." I hand him a sheet from the pad, which has the Jewel's address and phone number at the top. "If you want to write, that is. My mom won't let me have my own email account until I'm twelve." I feel like I'm in kindergarten. "Maybe you can send me a picture of you playing basketball."

He smiles and takes the paper. When his mother gets back to the car she folds up the wheelchair and puts it in the back seat. Her eyes are dull again, like the batteries are already drained.

"Say goodbye, Anton. We have a long drive."

Anton holds up his hand, palm facing me. I touch my palm to it. My fingers are small and skinny against his but they feel warm and tingly where we touch. His mother gets in, puts his window up and backs out of the space.

I watch until the car disappears around the corner.

Básquetbol en silla de ruedas.

That's how you say wheelchair basketball in Spanish.

I'm not sure what to do now that Anton's gone, so I go over to the diner. It's packed and smells like fresh muffins, which Mr. Whitley makes every morning. It's gotten so busy that he had to hire someone to help in the kitchen even though he didn't want to. He still cooks all the food himself but now he has someone to wash and cut vegetables and do stuff like grate cheese, boil macaroni, scrub the pots and run the giant dishwasher, which seems to be going all the time.

But I'm still the only one who gets to help with the pies.

Mrs. Whitley sets me up on a table in the corner with a huge pile of washed grapes and a big empty pot. I wash my hands and start popping. Pick up grape, squeeze, plop into pot. Pick up grape, squeeze, plop into pot.

It gives me time to think.

Pareidolia. Miracles. Jewish. Catholic.

I tried to ask Uncle Mordy why Mom has this thing about Catholics but he said I should talk to her about it. Which I haven't, given how well our discussion about Maria's necklace went.

Susan sits down across from me, startling me, and I send a zombie eyeball straight into her chin.

I can't even say sorry, I'm laughing so hard.

She reaches for the napkin holder, laughing too.

"I guess I deserve that for sneaking up on you again." It seems like the first time was a million years ago, but it's just been a few days.

175

"Did you get to interview a lot of people?" I ask.

"Three so far. And Father Donovan has been really helpful."

Mrs. Whitley delivers an armful of plates to the table across from us and then comes over.

"Wow, Miriam, you've gotten a ton done." To my surprise, my pot is almost half full. I think I could do this in my sleep.

"Go rest your fingers at a clean table and Mr. Whitley will make you some lunch." Mrs. Whitley turns to Susan. "How about you, Susan?"

Susan looks at a menu as we move to the next table over. "How about a Reuben? Haven't had one of those since I was a kid."

"One Reuben it is. And you, Miriam? Miriam Special or VBLT?"

"A VBLT sounds good, thanks, Mrs. Whitley." Even I can get tired of grilled cheese after a while.

In the booth on the other side of us are some people I don't recognize. I don't think they're staying at the Jewel. Some people come up just for the day if they don't live too far away, but it seems like everyone's heard about Mrs. Whitley's grape pie.

Susan's hair is wet. I'm not sure if it's from the shower or the pool.

"How do you do it?" I ask her.

"Do what?"

"Swim like you do."

She shrugs. "I grew up near the ocean, in California. We went to the beach all the time. The water is like a second home."

I can't imagine ever being that comfortable in it. I don't want to be afraid of water. I just can't help it. Maybe that's Mom's problem with Catholics. She doesn't feel comfortable around them. I just wish I understood why.

Mrs. Whitley arrives with a plate in each hand.

"One Reuben." She puts a steaming sandwich down in front of Susan. It looks like corn beef with cheese oozing out. Definitely not kosher.

"And one VBLT," she says, putting the second plate down in front of me.

"Thanks."

"VBLT?" asks Susan.

"Veggie bacon, lettuce and tomato," I tell her. Mrs. Whitley still thinks I'm a vegetarian, which I kind of feel bad about. The veggie bacon doesn't smell as good as the real thing, but it's still yummy.

As we eat, I decide I'll take a chance and talk to Mom. But this afternoon Kate is coming over. She says she wants to do something but wouldn't say what over the phone.

I just hope it doesn't involve water or heights.

"Let's go see it," says Kate.

"See what?"

"The apparition, obviously. What else is there to see in this town?"

"That's what you want to do today that you couldn't tell me on the phone?"

"Why not?"

"We know what it looks like. And besides, what if they catch us? Lekha's brother says police watch the crowds at fires because people who set fires like to stay and watch them burn."

"No one's going to catch us. And besides, we really didn't do anything wrong. You even said that, that the face was already there. We just got people to notice it."

I shake my head. "I don't know."

"And besides, look at all the good that's come from it. The motel is full and making money. Grandma can't make pies fast enough. Maria is working overtime and making even more money for school so she can go back and help all those people in Mexico. And you get to still live here."

"Yeah, and people are spending time and money to come from all over to see a Virgin Mary apparition that isn't real," I say. "Like Anton."

"Well, according to that para-whatever stuff you told me about, none of them are real."

Kate should be a lawyer.

"Let's go." She gets up and starts toward the diner where we keep the bikes.

I look for Mom to tell her I'm going biking with Kate but I can't find her. Maria's at the front desk and tells me that she and Dad are out at the hardware store.

It's just as well Mom's not here to ask me questions. She's already told me to stay away from the drive-in, which is pretty funny, considering.

"We don't believe in that stuff," she said.

I don't know what she's afraid of. But I know what I'm afraid of.

If she found out what Kate and I did, I think she'd explode.

The drive-in is no longer deserted. In fact, it's crammed. There are posts and rope set up like at an

179

amusement park, with people waiting in a zigzagging line. You don't have to pay, but there are stands selling sandwiches, chips, water and even souvenirs. There are statues of the Virgin Mary, paintings of the Virgin Mary and scarves with a Virgin Mary print. Even water bottles with the Virgin Mary on them.

And there are crosses. Lots of crosses. Big and small. Made of wood and plastic and metal. Chunky ones on strings of colorful beads. Delicate ones on silver chains.

Mom would have a heart attack.

I see families with little kids, old people, couples, people standing by themselves. People are smiling and talking to each other. It's like a big family reunion.

We drop our bikes and helmets under the tree at the edge of the lot. I follow Kate to the back of the line. An elderly couple gets in line behind us. The man is using a cane. The sun beats down on my head and I wish I'd brought some water.

I feel like people are staring at us, at me. Can they tell I'm Jewish?

I watch as people have their turn in front of the screen. Some take pictures, some point. Others kneel, or just stand totally still, staring at it. I'm too far away to hear if they're praying.

When it's finally our turn Kate pulls me over to the screen. This time when I look up, I don't see a face. I just see the cracks and the rust stain and the cross-shaped rips underneath. Kate doesn't say anything.

We walk off to the side and I turn to watch the couple behind us. They stand with their arms around each other. The man points and traces something in the air. The woman nods and smiles and I see tears roll down her cheeks.

I turn my head because it seems like a private kind of moment.

Kate is looking at the couple too.

We're quiet as we walk back to the bikes. As we head home, slower this time because of the heat, I can't make up my mind.

Is what we did bad or good? Yes, we fooled people, but if it makes them happy and gives them hope and saves the motel and the diner, is that so bad?

As we pass the gas station, Kate slows down and looks back at me. I shake my head. I'm not in a popsicle mood, even though sweat is dripping down my eyelids.

As we turn onto the Jewel's block, I see two police cars parked on the road up ahead. A bunch of people are gathered around the entrance to the parking lot.

Kate speeds up and I pump to catch up with her.

I ditch the bike and push my way through all the people milling around, talking in whispers. I don't recognize any of them and look for my parents or Uncle Mordy or Maria.

What is going on?

I hear Dad's voice and find him talking to a police officer.

"No," he says, "I have no idea who would do something like this."

Do something like what? I look around for Kate but can't find her. I try to get Dad's attention but he holds up his hand to say wait.

I check out the motel from where I'm standing, the first floor and then the second. A couple of people are standing on the balcony, looking down at us.

That's when I see it.

The Jewel's sign.

Dad takes my hand.

"Come, Miriam," he says, but my feet are cemented to the ground like they get in the pool. My eyes can't leave the sign.

There's a big black X painted over the *e* and *l* in Jewel. In the corners there are black crosses with the ends of the arms bent to the side. I've only seen them in books but I know what they are.

The No Vacancy sign underneath hangs down from one chain, the other side pulled off.

"Who would do that?" I whisper. My throat is tight and I feel dizzy.

"I don't know, Miriam," Dad says, putting his arms around my shoulders. "I don't know."

I look around at the people, the police officer, at the motel and the full parking lot, and then back at the sign.

The sign that now says The Jew Motor Inn, with ugly swastikas painted in each corner.

After the police are done interviewing my parents and taking pictures and inspecting for footprints and other clues, Uncle Mordy finds a big tarp in the storage closet. Kate and Sammy and I watch from Reception as he and Dad cover the sign with it and tie it down with string. Father Donovan walks over from the diner to help.

Mom comes in and gives me a long hug. "You okay?"

I'm not, but I nod yes. She busies herself on the computer, ignoring the phone, which keeps ringing and ringing.

Even Kate is quiet.

As they cover the sign, the sky gets darker and darker. There's a flash of light and a big clap of thunder and then rain comes pouring down. Dad and Uncle Mordy and Father Donovan run in. Sammy whimpers and hugs my leg. The lights flicker. I hope we have flashlights somewhere.

Mrs. Whitley walks over, without yoo-hooing like she usually does, and invites us to the diner. We all scurry over, holding our hands over our heads. The raindrops are so big and coming down so hard they hurt.

Father Donovan goes to sit in his usual booth and waves us to come join him. Kate goes right over. Mom gives him a stiff smile and heads to the big corner booth with Dad and Uncle Mordy. Sammy's hiding his face in Mom's shoulder. Mrs. Whitley is already pouring everyone mugs of coffee.

I'm not sure which table I want to sit at and stand there feeling like I'm the one who did something wrong.

Which is kind of true.

Is this punishment for what Kate and I did? My throat feels tight and lumpy when I swallow.

Mrs. Whitley comes over to where Father Donovan and Kate are sitting and puts two steaming mugs of hot chocolate on the table. She sits down and motions for me to join them. I look over at Mom and she nods.

"Feels more like a hot chocolate kind of day than a lemonade one," Mrs. Whitley says as I sit down.

Thunder cracks and I jump.

"I think God is showing his displeasure about the events of today," says Father Donovan. "Fire and brimstone and all that."

Mrs. Whitley's eyes are watery. "I'm really sorry, Miriam."

I'm surprised. "But it's not *your* fault."

"No, but I feel we all have a shared responsibility for the hate in the world. Your family has been nothing but welcoming to everyone coming to see the apparition, and it makes me sick that someone would do this awful thing."

I'm not sure my family has been exactly *welcoming*. And what would Mrs. Whitley think if she knew what Kate and I did? I feel Kate looking at me but I don't look up.

My hot chocolate has cooled off enough to drink but I'm not in the mood for it. I stir the spoon around and around, listening to the *clink, clink* as it hits the side of the mug.

I wake up after tossing around all night and look out the window. The rain has stopped and Maria is pulling the tarp off the sign. She's got the step stool and a bucket and starts scrubbing away at the swastikas with a big sponge. The first one comes off quickly but leaves a gray shadow like a ghost. I watch for a few minutes but don't go out to help. My stomach aches even more than during a swimming lesson.

Reception is empty but I can hear Dad on his cell phone in the office behind the desk.

"No comment," he says a few times and then hangs up. Mom, on the other hand, has a lot to say, at least to Dad. Neither of them hears the bell or notices me come in.

"What if it was someone staying here at the motel?" Mom says. "And to do something like that in broad daylight?" Her voice cracks. "Obviously no one tried to stop them."

Dad shakes his head. "This kind of vandalism only takes a few seconds. It was probably some bored kids who don't know any better. And they could be from anywhere."

"Give me a break, Daniel. This place is teeming with people who hate us."

"For goodness sake, Deb, do you hear yourself? Just because people are Christian doesn't mean they all hate Jews. Whoever did this disgusting thing doesn't know us. They're just ignorant."

The bell tinkles again behind me.

"Ignorant?" Mom raises her voice. "You're the one being ignorant. Have you read the newspapers lately? And how do you know it wasn't a guest, or someone who works here? Maria was in charge while we were out."

"I am not even going to entertain that." He sounds really angry now.

I turn to see who just came in. It's Maria, still holding the bucket. The water's black and the sponge is filthy.

Did she hear what Mom said? Her free hand starts to reach up to her necklace but then stops and drops to hang by her side.

Mom comes out of the office and sees Maria. Neither says anything. Then Mom rushes past her out the door. The *tinkle, tinkle* makes me want to scream.

Maria still doesn't say anything, just heads through the room toward the hallway. Some of the water sloshes out of the bucket onto her feet as she goes. Dad comes out of the office.

"Miriam —"

I pretend I don't hear him and follow Maria to the laundry room and watch her dump the bucket into the sink. The dirty water circles around the drain before it gets sucked down with a slurp.

Does Maria think I agree with Mom, that *she* could have done it? Or someone else at the motel? I'm glad Anton already left, although I guess Mom couldn't have accused him because he wouldn't have been able to reach that high.

I can't think of a single thing to say. Not in English. Not in Spanish. I don't even know who I'm mad at. I guess mostly the horrible person who did that to our sign.

There's a big pile of wet towels sitting on the floor, so I start loading them into the washing machine. I close the door to the machine as Maria puts the detergent into the compartment and then we both reach to press the Start button at the same time.

Her hand gives mine a squeeze. I squeeze back and then run out the door, not wanting to look her in the eyes.

15

It's been three days since the sign was vandalized. The day after, at Shabbat dinner, Dad looked sad and Mom jumped every time Sammy dropped his spoon or banged on the table. Even Uncle Mordy was serious.

That night I dreamed that I got locked in the storeroom in the dark and no one heard me calling to get out.

Dad came when he heard me cry out in bed and sat with me until I fell back asleep. Since then I've been having trouble falling asleep, even though I'm so tired.

Sammy's super clingy and has been sleeping on a mat on the floor next to Mom and Dad's bed. I don't like sleeping alone, even though the door to the outside is locked and the door between the two rooms is open.

The reporters have stopped calling. Uncle Mordy had someone come and repaint the sign, all professional looking, so you can't see the shadows anymore. They chose paint the color of red licorice for the letters, and I hate it.

It's Monday. Kate's mom is letting her skip camp today to hang out with me, but it's still early and she's not here yet.

The motel is just as full as always with people coming to see the apparition. But it's not the same. Before, it felt like everyone was on the same team. Now I feel like I'm dividing everyone into two groups in my head, like at color war at day camp last summer.

Blue team, red team. Catholic, Jewish.

The Catholic team is way bigger.

The best part of color war was the last night when we all stayed at camp until after dark. The counselors made a big bonfire and we cooked hot dogs and made s'mores. Then we all stood in a big circle around the fire with our arms around each other's shoulders and sang the camp song together.

In the dark, you couldn't tell who was wearing blue and who was wearing red.

Father Donovan's car pulls into the diner parking lot and I wait a few minutes to make sure he's not getting a coffee to go. When I go over, he's at his table with a bunch of papers laid out and a notebook that he's scribbling in. He's got his coffee, of course. There's a water bottle on the table with Catholic Library Association printed on it.

"Catholics have their own libraries?" I ask.

Father Donovan looks up.

"Oh, hi, Miriam." He looks at the bottle. "Yep. So do Jews. Your people may be called the People of the Book, but the rest of us like to read too."

He smiles and I know he's making a joke, but still, I think, *your* people? Aren't we all one people? Why does everyone keep talking about us and them?

It's like he reads my mind. "I'm sorry, Miriam. It's been a tough couple of days, hasn't it?"

"Yeah," I say, my eyes watering.

"Have time to sit down?"

I sit across from him but don't say anything.

He lets the silence sit there, like it's part of the conversation. I fold a napkin into smaller and smaller rectangles.

The quiet somehow makes me feel better. I wonder if this is what it feels like to go to confession.

I take a deep breath. "Kate and I faked the apparition. Sort of." I look down at the table so I don't have to look him in the eyes.

"I know," he says gently.

I look up. "You know?"

"I met with Officer Mike last week. Someone found this under the scaffolding at the drive-in." He pulls a Swiss Army knife out of his pocket and places it on the table. The initials B.W. are engraved in the red plastic.

Brendan Whitley. Kate's brother. We totally forgot to go back and look for the knife.

"Oh."

"Mike remembered that he saw you and Kate at the drive-in that morning. The morning he noticed the face on the screen. Wasn't too hard for him to put two and two together."

More silence. Then the diner door opens and Kate comes in. "Found you!"

She sees my face and sits down next to me.

"What's up?" she says, looking at me but not at Father Donovan.

I nod toward the knife.

"Oh," she says.

Father Donovan waits quietly, like he has all the time in the world.

I bite my lip.

"We needed to do something to save the motel," Kate finally says.

"And the diner, and Maria's job," I add. "And when we saw the face at the drive-in ..."

I stumble and Kate takes over. "We know it was wrong, but ..."

Kate stops talking and Father Donovan looks at her and then at me and the corner of his mouth twitches, just a little bit.

"You trespassed and destroyed property, and you intentionally tried to mislead a whole lot of people —"

I open my mouth, but he holds his hand up.

"But I think it's the face that people believe is the Virgin Mary, with or without the cross. I'm not saying that you and Kate didn't do something wrong, but as a result, you've done a lot of good around here. Officer Mike doesn't think he needs to report this to his superiors."

A whoosh of relief courses through me. Kate takes my hand and squeezes it.

Mrs. Whitley comes out. She looks us over like we're a menu, tilting her head first at Kate and then me and then Father Donovan.

"Don't worry, Myrna. All's good," he says.

"I guess I'll have to take your word on that," Mrs. Whitley says, looking unconvinced. "In any case, I need to borrow my granddaughter for a few minutes. Her mom's on the phone."

Kate follows her into the kitchen.

I feel so much better, until I remember the sign.

"Why do some people hate Jews?"

Father Donovan looks out at the cars in the parking lot for a bit before he answers.

"Have you ever made assumptions about something or someone but then found out you were wrong?"

The first thing I think of is the geodes at the Crystal Caverns store, how they look like ugly brown rocks on the outside but are beautiful jewels on the inside.

Then I think about when we got here and Mom thought that Maria couldn't speak English because she was from Mexico and had an accent.

And I think about Dahlia's big brother, Jonah.

The first time I met Jonah was a few weeks after Dahlia and I met in kindergarten and I went to her house to play for the first time. Jonah was in the kitchen with Dahlia's mom. He was waving his hands around and making grunting sounds. It was scary. I thought he was sick or something.

He wasn't sick though. He was deaf, and using sign language.

I don't tell Father Donovan any of this but I nod.

"When someone is different from us," he says, "sometimes we jump to conclusions instead of taking the time to understand."

I guess it's the same with Mom and Catholics.

"Have you been back to the drive-in?" he says.

I nod.

"What did you see there?"

"Nothing, really," I say, thinking of how I looked at the cracks and the stains but it didn't look like a face to me anymore.

"Not the screen. What else did you see?"

196

I remember watching the old man and woman standing next to me. I see in my mind how the man traced in the air with his finger and I see the woman's tears and how they stood with their arms around each other.

"Well," I say, trying to find the right words. "I guess I saw faith. And ... well ... love." I feel silly saying it, but it's true.

Father Donovan smiles. "Yes."

"But the swastikas ..." Mom may not like Catholics, but she would never do something like that.

Father Donovan sighs. "Yes, the swastikas." He takes my folded-up napkin and starts to unfold it. "What you did at the drive-in you did out of love. What someone did to your sign was done out of hate. At its worst, religion can make us hate each other, make us suspicious of people who believe differently from what we believe. But at its best, I believe religion can bring out the good in all of us."

He hands me the napkin to wipe my eyes.

"Be proud of who you are, Miriam, and don't let any ignoramuses with a paintbrush make you feel otherwise."

I can't talk because of the tears but that's okay. We just sit there until Mrs. Whitley comes over with a plate of French fries. I shake my head.

It's time to talk to Mom.

Mom and Dad are arguing in their room. I stand outside the door, listening through the crack.

"We're not moving back to the city, Deborah. That's ridiculous. Things are finally getting off the ground here."

"So?" Mom says. "We'll start over, at home."

"This is home now," he says.

"That stupid apparition. If it hadn't brought all these people here, this awful thing never would have happened."

"If there hadn't been an apparition, then we would have gone bankrupt a month ago."

Mom is crying.

"Listen, you know I'm not a religious person, not like Mordy, but I still think that sometimes things happen for a reason. Or maybe it's like the rabbi said. It's not what happens to us, it's what we do with what happens to us."

Mom makes a funny sound. "So what happened to me didn't matter?"

"That's not what I meant."

I push open the door.

"What happened to you?"

They look at me like I'm a ghost or something. Dad unfreezes first, gives Mom a gentle kiss on the cheek, says, "Talk to her," and goes out, giving me a squeeze on the shoulder.

I sit on the bed next to Mom.

"What happened to you?"

"It was a long time ago."

I sit quietly and wait, like Father Donovan.

She turns her hand palm out. The scar is faded but I can still make it out.

"I was twelve. Some older kids from the Catholic high school followed me home one day. They threw pennies at me and called me Jew-girl and when I ran, they chased me. I tripped and fell. I cut my hand open on some glass on the sidewalk. They stood over me. I thought they were going to …" Her voice trails off.

I put my hand on hers and trace the scar with my finger. It's a thin line about an inch long.

"That's horrible," I say. "Why would they do that?"

Mom stares at her hand. "I don't know, Miriam. I think I've spent my life since then trying to figure that out."

"What happened? How did you get away?"

"A car turned onto the street and the kids ran away. The driver asked if I was okay and I said yes and I went home and told Grandma and Grandpa I fell and cut my hand. They took me to the hospital for stitches and then everyone forgot about it. Everyone but me."

I let this sink in.

"Why didn't you tell them what happened?"

"I don't know. I guess I felt ashamed. Silly, huh?"

I shake my head, thinking about how I told Kate I was a vegetarian instead of telling her that bacon isn't kosher.

Mom looks out the window at the Jewel's sign. "I wonder if those kids ever thought about it after that. If they think about it now that they're adults. Because I do."

"How come you never told me about this before?"

She turns back to me. "I don't like to talk about it." She strokes my hair. "And I didn't want you to be afraid."

I squeeze her hand — one, two, three. I've really missed her this summer even though she's been right here.

"The worst part is that it's turned me into someone I don't like anymore," Mom says.

I think about the conversation I had with Father Donovan about jumping to conclusions and not taking time to understand people who seem different. The way I did with Jonah.

After I started hanging around at Dahlia's house, it just seemed normal to me that her brother talked with his hands. I even learned some signs so I could talk to him a little on my own.

I think about Anton too. He would have won that race, even if he hadn't cheated at the end. And I was sure he could never go faster with his wheelchair than I could run. Watching him in the pool, I realized that just because he uses a wheelchair doesn't mean that he can't do just about anything I can, and some things much better. I just needed to spend time with him to realize all that.

All of a sudden I know what to do.

"I love you, Mom." I give her a kiss and run to find Uncle Mordy, who lucky for me is by himself in the storeroom, flattening boxes. I explain my plan and he thinks it's a great idea. I run back to my room and grab the envelope from the top drawer, the one where I've been storing all the five-dollar bills Mrs. Whitley gives me.

As I close the drawer I see the little box that I keep my hamsa in.

I pull out the necklace and put it around my neck. I get the clasp to catch the first time. I turn back and forth in front of the mirror. It looks like it belongs there, the way Maria's cross belongs around her neck.

Uncle Mordy and I count the money together. One hundred and fifteen dollars!

"Is it enough?" I ask him.

"It's enough. But you don't have to use your own money. I can pay for the groceries. Are you sure you don't want to use it for something else? Something for you?"

This *is* for me. "I'm sure."

We figure out the details. It's already Wednesday, so we have only two days to get everything done. Uncle Mordy will do the shopping tonight and we'll start cooking tomorrow. We map out on paper how to put the tables together so that there will be enough seats for everyone. I spend the next hour on the computer making and printing enough invitations to put under all the room doors.

Four days until the Jewel Motor Inn's official Shabbat dinner.

16

We tell Mom and Dad that we're taking care of
Shabbat dinner this week and they don't need to
do anything and we want it to be a surprise so they
shouldn't ask questions. I tell Kate, of course, and
we let Maria in on everything, and Mrs. Whitley,
who, in addition to bringing over a gigantic bag of
potatoes and enough vegetables for a ginormous
salad, lends us a bunch of tablecloths and some
folding chairs she had in her basement.

On Thursday, Uncle Mordy, Kate and I make
five huge potato kugels. Kate's never even had potato
kugel, which Uncle Mordy says is unacceptable, and
cuts her a piece.

"This is so good," she says with her mouth full. "We need to tell Grandpa about it."

We lock the kugels in the motel fridge so my parents don't come across them. Mrs. Whitley comes over late at night and bakes some grape pies in our oven so that Uncle Mordy can eat them. Mom used to say back home that making Shabbat meals was like trying to feed an army.

And that was just for our family and guests!

On Friday I wake up to sunlight streaming in through the crack in my curtains. It's so bright out that I need to shield my eyes as I walk, still in my pajamas, across the parking lot and through the front office to get up to the kitchen. Uncle Mordy is whistling while he opens packages of cut-up chicken and lays the pieces in neat rows in a big pan. Forty-five minutes later we're singing together and cutting up carrots and tomatoes while the smell of baking brownies fills the air.

The bakery in Spartanburg delivers a big box of challahs along with the usual order of bagels. Maria's been checking with the guests and it looks like most of them are coming. Father Donovan says he'll be there, and all of Kate's family, even her brother.

I wish Anton were still here.

I take a break to get out of my pajamas and have a snack, taking a banana and cereal bar up to the balcony to sit with Maria during her break and go over my to-do list.

Before I've even peeled the banana, I hear noise on the stairs and Mom comes up. I quickly fold up the list and stick it under my leg.

"Have you seen Sammy?" asks Mom. She looks worried.

"Not since breakfast. Isn't he with the sitter?"

She shakes her head. "She couldn't come today. He's not with Uncle Mordy and your father just got back from town and ..." Her voice quavers. "He was with me earlier at the Reception desk and then the phone rang ... I'm going to check over at the diner."

Maria stands up. "We'll find him. Miri, you take the first floor and I'll check up here. *Vamos*. He's probably hiding away somewhere to escape from all the fuss."

I wouldn't blame him. At least being in the kitchen with Uncle Mordy I've gotten a break from all the stress around here.

I stick my head in the dining room on my way down to see if he's in there trying to reach the juice machine or playing with the salt shakers. The room is empty, and so is the laundry room at the bottom of the stairs.

I close my eyes and try to think where I last saw him. He was pouring syrup over a waffle at breakfast and making a big mess. He kept asking to go swimming, but Uncle Mordy told him he couldn't, because of all the —

A cold wave washes over me and I run toward Reception. The door to the pool is open.

He's not there. I'm so relieved I start to cry. But then I see a flash of color in the shallow end.

No! My brain shouts, but nothing comes out of my mouth.

He's at the bottom of the water, near the steps, his body a blur of blue shorts and yellow T-shirt, all wavy through the water.

"Sammy," I yell, finding my voice. "Sammy!" The blue and yellow blob doesn't move.

"Help!" I scream. "Help! Sammy's in the pool!" No one answers.

I've got to get him out. I step into the water, go right up to my waist. I shout at Sammy to move but he doesn't.

I can't breathe and my legs won't move. I force air into my lungs and tell my legs they have no choice and I throw myself off the step. My head stays above the water but I can't reach Sammy like that so I do it —

I go under, holding my breath and kicking my feet like Susan does.

It works. I reach out my hands and grab Sammy under the arms. Water fills my nose and mouth and I'm screaming Sammy's name underwater and then I stand up and pull him up to the surface.

"Sammy, Sammy," I'm yelling as I drag his limp body up the pool steps. He's so heavy out of the water and I don't think I can get him out and then all of sudden Uncle Mordy's there, and Mom and Dad and Maria.

Uncle Mordy lays Sammy down next to the pool and starts pushing on his chest while Dad yells into his phone for an ambulance. Mom kneels by Sammy's head, saying his name over and over and over. I stand there shivering and dripping and I think I'm going to throw up.

I run for the door, right into Mrs. Whitley. She takes one look at the scene inside and at the water dripping off me and scoops me up in her strong arms and buries my face in her shoulder. She somehow carries me out to Reception and sits down on the couch. She hugs me and rocks me back and forth and tells me it's going to be okay.

My eyes are closed but I can see Sammy's still white face lying on the blue tile floor and I'm not sure it's going to be okay.

I scrunch my eyes even tighter together.

And I pray.

17

The hospital is so quiet. Everyone seems to talk in whispers. Above all that silence is the *beep-beep-beep* of the machines that are supposed to be helping people get better.

We sit in a little room next to a pair of electric doors that go into the ICU, where they are taking care of Sammy. I know why they call it a waiting room. That's all we've been doing. Waiting.

I've only been in a hospital once before, to visit Grandpa after he had surgery on his knee. That time everyone was smiling and Grandpa was making jokes about climbing Mount Everest and asking Grandma to sneak him in donuts because he didn't like the hospital food.

The only smiles here are the stiff, fake kind.

Sammy hasn't woken up. He's only allowed to have two adult visitors at a time. But Uncle Mordy explains what happened and the nurse lets me go in. Dad takes me into the room, holding my hand tight. Mom is sitting next to the bed, stroking Sammy's cheek. She looks up and reaches her hand out to me.

My little brother looks so tiny on the big hospital bed, with a tube in his mouth and a bunch of thin tubes attached to his arms. The nurse says I can talk to him if I want to, that maybe he can hear me, so I put my face up to his ear.

But then I can't think of anything to say, so I take his hand and squeeze it — one, two, three — and I kiss his little cheek.

Dad talks in a low voice to a doctor in the hallway and then takes me back to the waiting room before he goes back in to Sammy's room. It feels like the clock on the wall has stopped. There are some other people here who must be waiting too, hoping that the person they love will be okay.

I lie down across two of the chairs with my head in Uncle Mordy's lap, and reach up and turn my hamsa around between my fingers.

I must fall asleep because when I wake up Uncle Mordy's moved to a chair and there's a blanket over me. I sit up and can see the sun low in the sky through the window at the far end of the room. Mom and Dad are both in the waiting room, leaning against each other.

"How's Sammy?" I whisper.

"He's moving around a little, starting to wake up," Dad says. "It's a good sign." He squeezes Mom's shoulder. "The nurses are changing shifts and they asked us to go out for a bit."

There's some noise in the hallway and I look over and see Father Donovan coming down the hall toward us. Dad goes to meet him and they talk quietly for a few moments. Dad looks back at me and Mom and then nods at Father Donovan, who heads back the way he came.

And then he's coming back, leading a group of people carrying bags and packages.

Mr. and Mrs. Whitley.

Maria and Susan.

The couple who owns the gas station down the street and the guy who sells us popsicles.

Kate and her brother, with her parents right behind them.

Everyone pours into the room, and now I see the bakery guy and the man who cleans the pool. And guests from the motel. Lots of guests. People keep crowding in. I think maybe the whole Jewel is here.

Father Donovan sets his bags down and I see challahs sticking out of them. Someone else has a tinfoil tray of chicken. I see the potato kugels and my brownies.

"I hope we're not intruding," Father Donovan says, "We thought you could use your community at a time like this."

Mom starts to cry. Dad reaches for her hand.

I look around at all the worried faces. Our community.

Somehow there's enough room for everyone. People sit on the other couches or the chairs along the sides of the room. Some stand. Susan and Kate sit on the floor.

Father Donovan pulls something out of one of his bags and sets it on the counter across from the couch. It's two little lights made to look like candles. He shows me how to flip a switch underneath them, and the tiny bulbs at the top flicker like flames.

"Rabbi Yael sent them. No real candles allowed in the hospital," he says. He takes a plastic cup and a bottle of grape juice out of the bag. Maria pulls out two challahs and arranges them on a plate.

I throw myself into Father Donovan's arms, crying. He bends down and whispers into my ear, "You are so brave, Miriam. Like your namesake. She saved her brother too."

In the Torah, Miriam saves her baby brother, Moses. That makes me cry harder.

He gives me a hug and a tissue and motions toward the window where the sky is getting dimmer. "Hurry."

I pull Mom over to the candles.

I put my hands over my eyes and wait for Mom to say the blessing. Her voice is quivery so I join her:

Baruch atah, Adonai Eloheinu, Melech Haolam, asher kidishanu b'mitzvotav v'tzivanu l'hadlik ner shel Shabbat.

Blessed are You, Lord Our God, King of the Universe, who has sanctified us with His commandments, and commanded us to light the lights of Shabbat.

I say an extra prayer to myself for Sammy and then turn around.

Father Donovan takes Dad's hand in his and then holds his free hand out to Maria. She takes it, and offers her other hand to Uncle Mordy. The ripple of hands moves from one person to another, the people sitting raising their hands to meet those who are standing and back down again. Mom takes my free hand in hers.

A kind of silent hum takes over the room. It's a vibration that seems to come from everyone's hearts rather than their mouths.

Some people have their eyes closed and some look at the floor or at the candles. Mom catches Maria's eye and they smile at each other, even though both of them are crying. Kate looks right at me and hugs me with her eyes.

The room is still and quiet and at the same time bursts with energy.

It's as if everyone is praying, each in their own way.

But for the same thing.

18

I'm on my back, eyes closed. I count out loud to ten, real slow, "… eight … nine … ten."

Next to me, Dahlia and Lekha start to cheer. "You did it! You did it!"

Water splashes into my face and I roll onto my front. Even though I'm wearing floaties, I grab the railing of the ladder at the side of the deep end. Kate does a somersault underwater and comes up next to us.

I love seeing Kate and Dahlia and Lekha together, even if it's just for a few days.

At the shallow end, Sammy paddles around in his water tube. Dad dives underneath him, making him giggle and shriek. He's totally fine, and not the least bit afraid of the water, even though it's been only two weeks since he almost drowned. The doctors at the hospital said it was a miracle.

A real one.

Through the open door, I hear Mom and Maria in Reception, laughing as they go through carpet samples, trying to find something that matches the couches and will hide the dirt from all the feet that walk through.

Uncle Mordy went home last week to get ready for his classes. And even though Maria has a boyfriend again, a nurse she met at the hospital when Sammy was there, she and Uncle Mordy plan to talk on the phone once a week so he can practice his Spanish.

It's Friday. School starts next week.

New kids, new teachers. Homework and tests.

But today there's swimming. And hanging out with my three best friends.

"Yoo-hoo!" I hear through the pool door.

And a grape pie to make for Shabbat dinner.

ACKNOWLEDGMENTS

Like Miriam, community has always been very important to me, and I'm blessed to belong to so many of them.

To my literary community: thank you to Vermont College of Fine Arts and to Sarah Aronson for getting me there. To my VCFA class, the Darling Assassins, for keeping me there. To Sarah Ellis, the late Bonnie Christensen, and Shelley Tanaka, the VCFA advisors who read the very first incarnations of this book and told me to keep writing it. To critique partners and beta readers Susan You-Are-Awesome Korchak, Monica Roe, Katia Rania, Anna Craig, David Rogers, Sarah Aronson, Meg Wiviott, Francisco Stork, Gail Baker and Adam Sol. To Lyn Miller-Lachmann and Nicolle Lustgarten for checking my Spanish. (Any remaining mistakes are my own.) To Semareh Al-Hillal and the entire team at Groundwood, my newest community, for believing in this book, and to Sam Kalda for his perfect cover.

To my agent, Jacqui Lipton at Raven Quill Literary Agency, and Storm Literary. Another thank you to Shelley Tanaka — advisor, mentor, friend and now, editor. How lucky is that?

To my Jewish community: thank you for nourishing my body and soul for as long as I can remember.

To my friends and family, the most important community of all: thank you to Lisa Robinson, friend, colleague, and fellow second-career writer, for her cheerleading. To Shirley Katz — you know why. To Miriam Fangot, for keeping it all together. Thank you to my parents and sister for everything — I love you guys! To my in-laws, for the unwavering confidence. And most importantly, thank you to my husband, Jay, and my three children, for helping me make time to write and for seeing me as a writer before I did. That was probably the most important part.

TZIPORAH (TZIPPY) COHEN was born and raised in New York and spent eighteen years in Boston before landing in Toronto, where she now lives with her husband, three kids, two cats and one dog. Many years after graduating from Harvard Medical School, she received an MFA in Writing for Children and Young Adults from Vermont College of Fine Arts. She now splits her time between writing and working as an oncology/palliative care psychiatrist. Visit her at tziporahcohen.com and follow her on Twitter @tzippymfa.